THE CAPTAIN'S BASTARD

BOOK TWO OF THE ACCIDENTAL PIRATES SERIES

MICHAELA ALLEN

Illustrated by LICARTO @99DESIGNS

Edited by BETH WONG

Edited by JOY ALLEN

Printed in New Zealand by Your Books https://www.yourbooks.co.nz

❀ Created with Vellum

This book is dedicated to S & M for your love, humour and a safe place. It is also dedicated to I, A and M for treating me like just another sister.

RECAP – THE BONNY PIRATES

The Bonny pirates started with our not so fearless heroine going about her usual business, you know rescuing handsome slaves for the position of cabin boy and pretending to be a bloodthirsty pirate. Anyway, right when she was looking forward to some rest, she was thrust into an adventure of monumental proportions. A land-based pirate funeral, some scare tactics and some well-timed information ensued. Chasing an enemy who is hellbent on destroying her, she set out on a mission to the beautiful city of Astrom in the land of Sirillia. What were the outcomes of our heroine's grand adventure? None other than finding out that her best friend Meena and Daughter Piper were princesses, and what do you know, her ship can fly. After saving the day, Morgan is mortally wounded, suspiciously she manages to survive, and when she awakes, she is rewarded for her efforts with a new Barony and a piece of wood. So, all in all, Morgan overcame the perils with her new beau, a god or two and her sword in hand. Read onwards for the next exciting instalment of Morgan's adventures.

PART ONE – ON THE BACK FOOT

DIVING IN

An unseasonable rain was sweeping through the area. The gentle calming sounds of water trickling through the limestone channels gave Arew a comforting feeling and brought a spring to his step. Water was scarce; like most cities in Sirillia it flowed from the distant mountains and ended up in channels cut from stone, wood and nature. The channels directed the life-giving resource towards the centre of the city, like the people that spent their days there it stopped only briefly to pool in the fountains and then quickly went about its business. After the water filled the fountains, it disappeared underground, where it filled the city's cisterns before being distributed to outlying dwellings. Water wasn't wasted, if it hit a surface it usually found its way to the channels. That was why, when Arew came across a gaggle of young children carelessly dancing in the rain and needlessly splashing in the puddles, he aimed a kick at the nearest waif for wasting such a precious resource with trivial merriment. And thus his internal mumblings began. It was bad enough the supposed free folk of Sirillia had gone from being dictated to by Tornbaer, now they were under the thumb of the Master's far-reaching oppression. The Master's cronies of various types treated all as if they were not originally Sirillian themselves; their dead-eyed stares were a constant indicator that the people were not thought of or cared about in any way. No aspect of their lives was untouched, even the flow of water was decreasing, all knew not to ask questions or stand up to the oppression. Life had always been cheap in the land of sand and sun, but now it was quite simply unbearable.

After arriving at his stall in the fish area of the market, Arew went about his task grumbling in a nonsensical manner as he set up his wares; because it wasn't fish which he sold It was essential to handle most of his powders and especially volatile potions with care. Now, Arew thought of himself as an honest and upfront type, and of course, all of his dealings were above board, which is why, when the hooded cronies walked up to his stall, he was surprised and slightly offended that they could be looking for a blameless type such as himself. Perhaps it was his very innocence that had got him into trouble. He, however, didn't have time to ponder further. Instead of the typical shakedown, he was shoved to his knees, and his hands were tied behind his back. The proceeding days weren't pleasant for him, he was beaten starved and least it is forgotten, verbally abused until he gave up a tiny and insignificant piece of information, nothing really, just information on the purchase of a dozen barrels of Dragon's Fire. For his troubles, even after he was so forthcoming, they continued to torture him until he forgot who he was and wanted to die, then finally sweet nothing.

MONTHS later somewhere in the vast Dantallo Desert:

It hadn't been a pleasant few weeks for Aiden, he had been captured, rescued, slept roughly mostly on the saddle and chased through miles of endless desert. Castain was his usual, silent, brooding self, with a tinge of added grumpiness on the side. He lifted his face cover over his mouth so he could be heard above the sounds of their horses and another insignificant sandstorm and nearly choked on heat-blasted sand for his efforts. His tone was brisk to suit his mood, "Oh come on, you can't still be bristly because I got captured. How was I supposed to know, she had a betrothed and a mean right hook?" Castain's only response was to stare towards the horizon and emit a noncommittal grunt. Not one to quit while he was ahead he asked, "How far from the coast are we do you think? I could do with a strong drink, I haven't had anything but water or camels milk since that barn we slept in." As no reaction was forthcoming, he continued, "Plus I'm sure my horse could do with some water as well."

Finally, he got a reaction, Castain's spun around stern façade affixed his retort was delivered in a typically brisk way, "One, the answer is the same since the last time you asked, approximately two days." Castain continued, raising his voice and lifting his mouth cover for effect, "And two, for the hundredth time we are not, taking your damn horse with us." Continuing to stare sternly for a second, Castain then turned back around, to face the gathering sandstorm in front of them.

Warily eyeing the storm, Aiden said emphatically, "But seriously, we have to take Prancer with us, this is the best horse I've had, and its stolen Castain, stolen!"

"A horse is a means to an end, what red-blooded man calls their horse Prancer, usually your horse's name is a reflection of you," Castain replied gruffly, not bothering to turn around. Castain hesitated and then continued, "On second thoughts Aiden, that's a perfect name for your horse." He was sure there was an upward lilt in Castain's voice as if he was smiling; he was not offended, their banter usually went on as such, they both had mutual respect, although Castain seemed to hide it well. He was sure at times that Castain disliked him, then he would realise it simply was not possible.

"How can you call yourself of Tornbaern royal blood with comments like that?" He re-joined.

"I've never claimed to be a good example of such, nor have I ever wanted to be," Castain replied calmly, not skipping a beat.

As the day wore on, Aiden kept his companion entertained, by outlining all the reasons why horses were amazing creatures. He was mid-comment on the breeds that were used at the Gatehouse, when a glance behind revealed an ominous cloud of dust, its size and shape indicating a large party of riders approaching with speed. A firm press to Prancer's sides promptly brought him beside Castain, who understand instantly and before they knew it, they were galloping in the direction of Astrom, which suddenly seemed much too far away. Before long Castain motioned with his hand towards a sandstorm coming in from their left. The grit depositing, pore shredding, wall of sand was an example of something they usually avoided. Knowing it would enable them to hide, he followed his companion. The heat, the danger, the bristly woman, yes it was safe to say he was over this mission, the sooner they got back to the Ship, the better. The well-stocked, newly commissioned Serpent was cleverly hidden in a cove, on the Farthing Cliffs to the East of Astrom.

It wasn't long before every bit of his uncovered skin was burning, and despite feeling turned around, his companion seemed to know where they were going. Onwards they went through blinding walls of sand, eventually in reprieve, hot day faded into the chilly night. As there were no longer signs of pursuit they slowed to rest their horses. Forward they continued thus, weary atop their saddles, hugging themselves for warmth, tiredly looking behind for signs of the chase.

Finally, on the second day amongst visible lines of heat and fading light, a blissful sight greeted them. Small columns of smoke rose into the air from a decidedly sleepy and welcoming looking Astrom. Although it confirmed they were to the west of the city away from the desired eastern approach, the sight lifted their spirits, nonetheless. Castain glanced behind to give one of his rare smiles, and it was as he reciprocated that their hopes were cruelly dashed by sounds of chase quickly approaching from the rear. There was no skirting the expansive garden city, they needed the streets and terraces to waylay their pursuers and it was the most direct route to their destination. With the possibility of capture at the forefront of their minds, they firmly pressed their horse's sides. They both knew what capture would bring; neither wanted to come under the Master's sway, or be killed because of their lack of usefulness. The stolen horses were fine specimens, their previous owner; a wealthy desert trader must have been very unhappy to find his well-trained beasts missing. As it turned out, their opportunistic decision was a fortunate one because their pursuers made no initial headway, their horses keeping a breakneck speed as desert gave way to sandy streets. An eyesore, the garrison soon towered over them, and they raced onwards, then down a tier, they descended, where the new lights of multi-levelled houses greeted them. The sandy streets changed into paved cobbles, yet more speed was employed as their horse's hooves created an eerie echo in the early darkness. Before long they were headed downward into yet another area of the city. Just as Aiden was beginning to feel like the whole experience was relatively anticlimactic, things got real. A wall of torches sprung up before them, accompanying the wall, a group of well-armed kingdom soldiers. Feeling like the welcome wagon was well and truly being brought out, he quickly followed Castain's down a side alley, the beautiful creature beneath him retaining the pace. It was as they neared the end of said alley, that the boom sounded. A shot from one of the city's newly installed anti-ship cannons efficiently and spectacularly destroyed a house above them. The result was pieces of house flying around them and despite the fact he did not shy, Prancer displayed fear in suddenly bulging eyes. Although he rarely swore, profanities slipped from Aiden's lips. Amidst destruction of home and property they continued onwards, finding more urgency in fear. It wasn't until they neared the entrance to another level on the upward east side, that another well-reinforced blockade sprung up before them. Making a quick and smart decision, smart considering the well-armoured wall of garrison soldiers before them, they veered into another ally. Everything was happening with breakneck speed, instinct his only guide. Riding into a trap, a row of armoured garrison men greeted them, and their exit was quickly blocked by similarly armed types. Putting his faith in Castain, he ducked below his horses head to create a smaller target and followed into a small courtyard. Cornered their only option was forward, and so forward they went, spurring their horses over the courtyard wall, as the road below met hooves, the substantial drop was too much for Castain's horse which slowed to a limp then stopped, halting all progress. Aiden spun Prancer around and came alongside. Holding out his arm Castain took it and was quickly hoisted behind him. As they galloped away, he envisaged the beautiful white mare getting enveloped by a swarm of soldiers; the image gave his heart a pang, such a faithful and majestic creature did not deserve such treatment, and they were the perpetrators. Onwards they sped, not surprisingly once they had enough distance on the solders the booms started up again. It was evident that the operators of the cannons had no thought for the lives of the people nor did they care about the ruining of livelihoods. Thankfully, when they reached the eastern edge of the city freedom became a reality.

Castain called into his ear, "Get off the road, it's too well lit, they will have a clear shot." Confused by the comment he froze. Castain grabbed the reins, veering them sharply towards a sprawling mansion located on the very edge of the city, the courtyard and a central garden quickly blazed past them with Castain steering the horse straight as an arrow. He was confused by Castain's intentions at first, yet understanding came in the form of action. The walls of most of the houses were made from a mix of sand and clay, as his horse's force and weight hit the surface they were soon inside the mansion. There was a split-second view of a rotund merchant bemusedly staring up from his bed, then they made it through another wall and into the open beyond. Another swift kick sent Prancer towards full speed, not a moment too soon, the house behind was promptly destroyed by cannon fire. Only a moment was spared for thoughts of the once beautiful mansion. Aiden then directed them towards The Serpent and safety.

They continued in a deliberate zig zag ensuring the cannons could not find their target until they made it over a raise, it was then that Castain called in his ear, "We have company and a lot of it, concentrate on riding." At that Castain switched his position to face the oncoming riders, his thighs keeping him astride. Aiden was not able to see the scene behind him although, he knew from the noises and bouts of pressure upon his back, that not only was Castain inflicting causalities, but the enemy was close at hand. It hurt, but for good measure he kicked Prancer once again to receive anything else that he had to give, never disappointing his faithful steed rewarded him with more speed. Feeling a surge of pride for his horse, he concentrated on the terrain in front of him.

Soon they were skirting the Farthing Cliffs, the noises and pressure upon his back, told him Castain had run out of arrows and was using his sword to ensure no attackers got through. After a strangled cry, which he assumed was from Castain throwing a dagger, he felt his companion spin back around. Once secure upon the saddle Castain called into his ear, "There are too many of them, your horse can't take much more of this, there is only one option now."

Confused he had no idea what Castain meant, the dots did not connect until his counterpart grabbed the reigns and directed Prancer sharply towards the dangerous and suicidal cliffs. Not skipping a beat Prancer took them full tilt over the precipice, for a moment he could see the surreal image of his horse's hooves in a beautiful arc as if they were simply executing a jump. Two words came out of his mouth as they plummeted towards the water below, "PRANCER NOOOOOOOOOOOO."

The drop seemed to take forever; he even had enough time to ponder the sheer trust of the animal Castain had sent over the cliff. As horse and riders separated mid-air, there was no control or way of dodging the arrows which their pursuers fired at them. When an arrow struck him, he could do nothing but continue to fall. Finally, when he hit, the sharp cold water took everything from him, including his breath, his thoughts, and his senses. A dark sinking coldness greeted him.

OLD FRIENDS NEW ENEMIES

He had only been back at the Citadel a little over a month and was still adjusting to the need for formality and pomp, not that he ever wanted to leave in the first place. His father had sent him away to the Plains, with malicious awareness of the fact he enjoyed his life here. Rollston was quiet and sleepy compared to the bustle around him. It was not the restrained, snobbish well-oiled Citadel of his youth, the Commons was open, and just like the colourful tapestries a blend of people, mixed with a carefree air, that was until his footfalls met the long hall. His very presence changed the atmosphere from harmony to discord. Greeted with guarded stares and hidden whispers, he was, as always reminded being a noble's bastard was hard at the best of times, but being the bastard of Fife Dallinger the most hated noble in the kingdom, combined with his newly elevated status was maddening. Despite the fact he did not usually care what others thought of him, he was a target for hatred, disdain and most annoying of all, mistrust. Squaring his shoulders, he pointedly told himself for the hundredth time since he had arrived, that he was not his father's son, nor did he even know what it meant, to be such. Contemplating a return to Rollston and self-imposed exile, he pushed aside the thought, sighed and continued to walk, one forced step after another. After making his way into the throne room he patiently waited to be introduced, watching his friend listening to a supplicant, he was as always reminded of Leo's ability to set one at ease and listen deeper than merely with one's ears. He had spent most of his teenage years playing swords and hunting with Leo, so he knew that his friend was a different more serious and sometimes sad version of the boy he once knew. As the supplicant walked away, Leo eyes fell upon him, and although he did not receive a smile, a familiar twinkle belied his friends underlying esteem. The announcement of his name caused all stares to turn as if magnetized towards him, "I present His Grace, Hector James Dallinger, the Duke of Rollston, Your Majesty."

Bowing as his name continued to echo off the walls of the throne room, he waited to be addressed; instead, Leo stood and announced in a business-like manner, "That will be all today." Leo moved purposefully in his direction, "walk with me, Hec." He asked politely.

Falling in behind, Hector followed waiting for his friend to talk, it was clear, Leo wanted to have a private conversation, he had a fair idea of its serious nature purely because they walked in silence until they entered the Royal apartments. Once there, however, in a hurried senseless rant, words tumbled out of Leo's mouth, "I'm sorry about that, I know how you hate all that stuff, with your appointment as the new Duke of Rollston you will have to get used to it. Ah, as you can appreciate, there are eyes on you, a lot of tongues wagging and all that."

Although he was happy to let Leo continue, he was now a little worried about the tone of the rant, apprehensive he interrupted, "Are you getting to the point at any stage?"

Leo looked almost embarrassed, and he continued haltingly, "Yes ah, it's just that, you are spending way too much time with my betrothed, do I need to be worried?"

It was usual for Hector to be the serious broody type. So he applied his usual abruptness, in his pointed reply," Firstly, congratulations on your betrothal. Secondly and with all the respect due in which our friendship allows, Are you telling me, you of all people, are believing the lies, if that's the case I am indeed a busy man, the other twenty ladies, courtesans and commoners, who I am bedding keep me such." Seeing Leo look sheepish, he felt terrible and continued, in a more respectful tone, "we are friends, you know that Bella and I grew up alongside one another until I was sent away to be your companion." Taking a breath to calm himself, he continued, "do you trust me, Bella, and most importantly yourself?"

Leo's reply was without hesitation, "Yes."

Heartened by his friend's demeanour, he said, "Then do me a favour and remember, I have always been and will always be loyal to you, and secondly to the crown of which it happens, you are both." After he had finished placating Leo, they spent the afternoon openly discussing the things only their friendship allowed.

That afternoon, as he walked back to his quarters, deep down a worry surfaced that he was ignoring his true feelings despite his best intentions, that worry like others of its kind, got pushed down to a place where he could do his duty and protect his friend.

SHE FOUND FIRING ARROWS CATHARTIC, and right now she needed it, from cheek to nocking point, to target, the recurve bow enabled a release of stress and arrow. One after the other they hit the centre of the target. Aside from immersing herself in the historical records, of which the library afforded a vast array, this was Bella's favourite pastime. At her side Darren and Randall, two of her finest archers and aside from Hector her only citadel-based friends. It was of course, ok to forget, that they were all more loyal to the crown than her. She found herself needing to get out of the Citadel more and more these days, especially as Mira's treatment of her had escalated to unfortunate proportions. She was mild in manner, but without the thrum of the string, she was sure she would have cracked under pressure long ago, if it weren't for her all-consuming love for Leo, she would have gone to find her real friends to vent her frustrations. It was that thought that left her wondering what Morgan and crew were up to, probably playing Captains Bastard or rescuing some surprised damsel or rather, she envisioned the damsel surprised of course because the rescue came from a crew, mostly made up of beautiful woman. The sound of Leo's voice did what it always did, lifted her spirits and brought a smile to her face, "Now that's what I needed to see." Turning her smile in his direction, she watched the broad framed, blonde-haired, blue-eyed love of her life strolling assuredly towards her.

Bowing she waited for her compatriots of the bow to politely walk away before replying to the sadness she saw behind Leo's eyes, "don't tell me, the nobles are still giving you a hard time about elevating Hector to their snowy heights?"

Raising an eyebrow, he replied sheepishly, "Yes, that and so many other things. I want to ask you a favour, but I know you are not going to like it."

She responded hesitantly, "Ok, I'm all ears, I think."

Leo's reply was tinged with worry, "When Sha and I, leave tomorrow for the hunting trip, I need you to stay here."

Her stepmother had taught her, if you didn't have anything nice to say, don't you dare say anything at all, so she picked up her bow and started firing. The thwack of arrows hitting the target considerably louder than before he arrived. Leo's hand resting upon her shoulder brought calm, and so did his words, "My mother will come around. That is why I need you to stay, we will be away a month, and if she doesn't come round before I return, then it won't matter, because I will be announcing our engagement to the court, whether we have her blessing or not."

Lowering the bow in shock, she looked to Leo, the seriousness on his face ensuring she dropped the only thing that meant more to her, than him. Gently picking up her bow, he placed it between them before sealing his declaration with a kiss. As he proceeded to hold her out at arm's length, her tears must have given him pause because he spoke, as if he could read her thoughts, "Ignore your stepmother's voice and listen to me, I love you and only you, nothing will change that fact. No more are you going to put me off, inferring you are not good enough for me. If anything Bell, it is I, who is not good enough for you. Please say yes."

Still trying to keep her tears at an acceptable level, she surprised herself by replying shakily, "That depends, is your mum part of the package?" His laugh made her heart soar, and they spent the rest of the afternoon connecting, be it words, hands or lips. Prolonging the moment until they had to part. They watched the sunset together. In a moment of perfect pastel brilliance, the calm sea of clouds in front of them formed breakers in the sky. The breakers stretching to the horizon and beyond.

Feeling forlorn Bella watched Leo leave, despite him having an early ride for the hunt, like a snapped sail rope, the contact broken left her unsure. Her day had swung from restrained pleasantness to unrestrained happiness, the safety of her bed called, falling into the feathered comfort, a smile upon on her face as she drifted into anon.

. . .

BELLA HAD an overwhelming desire to ride out to join Leo and Sha in their hunt. After three weeks her nerves and patience were frayed irreparably, it wasn't just the daily lectures about how a lady should act, etiquette and expectations, it was that they were delivered down the nose and under the guise of generalization. Bella had been summoned to the royal apartments, for just such, a one-sided conversation. Mira's first utterance, at her entrance, was, "A lady must have good breeding, my son will marry a high born, well-mannered lady, there are a few fine examples of such in the North."

It was all Bella could do to keep her head bowed and needlework consistent, the fine lace hanky in her hands shaking as her stepmother screamed in her head, "DON'T YOU DARE OPEN YOUR MOUTH, YOU WORTHLESS WELP." Yet something long held back snapped, standing she spoke in an impassionate tone. Yet, the meaning was in the body language and words, "Your son, will marry whom he chooses, I'm sure you wouldn't judge nonetheless. What was it your goddess teaches about judgement, to judge is to embrace an asp." Smartly choosing to walk away, she politely bowed and ignored the look of shock upon Mira's face, as she made a hasty exit.

Her steps took her to her room, and it wasn't long before she was donned in her uniform, the green leather was more than just armour, it was reassurance. A short time later, she was purposefully stepping out into the courtyard, the suns brightness made her blink, the weight of her bow a comfort against the warring thoughts in her head. It was as she was entering the training grounds, banging her palm upon her head, that she came across Hector and his apt comment, caused her to drop said palm in surprise, "Oh dear, has she been at it again?"

Sighing, she stood beside him and in reply loosed a few arrows; the twang soon calmed her and anxiety lifted. Typically, Hector was not bothered by her silence and simply continued to shift through his movements similarly, the muscles in his arms moving to the slices and sweeps in precision. After a while, Hector put up his sword and rested his shield, to stop and watch the arrows which were now hitting dead centre and forcefully splitting the previous. For a man, who was the broody silent type Hector seemed to want to talk, his uncharacteristic and thoughtful comment caused her to slowly undraw, "Look, she doesn't mean it, she is the most fiercely loyal woman I know, kind of like you, she will come around." She turned to take him in, his shield in front as if protection from his thoughts was offset by the backdrop of a halo caused by the suns glare. There it was, anguish and loss before now it had been easy to pretend his feelings weren't there. Continuing in deliberate ignorance of what was written upon his face, Hector tried to lighten the mood with familiar banter, "Besides, us bastards, should stick together."

She was about to reply to her gruff curly haired companion when for some reason, he stepped towards her and yelled uncharacteristically. Time slowed, as Hector yelled and planted his shield on the ground, she instinctively followed his order and knelt behind. She had enough time to realize he had protectively placed his arm around her before the blast hit. The force of the blast impacted upon Hector's shield, throwing them into the air, and it was as they spun in preparation to hit the ground, that she got her first glance of their attacker. Beneath the cowl of his black robes, his lips chanted, hands moving, between the dark energy grew in a spine chilling fashion. When their feet meet the ground, Hector yelled "MOVE," She was already in full flight, aware that dark energy would be hurled at her any second. She turned to confront her attacker head-on, screaming at him in defiance she raised her bow, all the while readying herself for a dive, yet before she could execute, Hector's shield collided with the side of the hooded one's head, and he crumpled to the ground. Without speaking, they raced to the cover of a set of wooden stands which over-looked the training grounds and as they came around the corner where the path met the courtyard, another dark caster greeted them. This one's face exhibited a cruel smile; clearly, he enjoyed his work. The caster proceeded to viciously hurl dark bolts towards them. The only available action was to cower behind the stands. A splinter caused face stinging pain as wood exploded around her. Biding her time, she loosed an arrow in between blasts, only to see it bounce off an invisible wall. As she ducked back behind the stands, another bolt of darkness grazed her, swearing from the searing pain of her skin burning, she was left with no option but to take cover and cower as step by step the attacker moved towards their hiding spot. Clenching her teeth in seething anger, she readied herself for one last seemingly useless stand. Gripping her bow firmly she squeezed Hector's shoulder to indicate her intent to attack, she stepped forward, at the same time, a yelp proceeded a crunching noise, and the hooded figure came flying past them, his end was to land lifeless on the ground. It was a familiar friendly voice that uttered blissful words, "You can come out, he's dead." Bob looked rather pleased with himself, although the horse he had used to charge the attacker, was rather terri-fied. Continuing for effect, Bob proclaimed, "Just admit it, you love me, and the horse I rode in on."

Instead of replying, she looked to Hector, and in unison, they exclaimed, "Mira." Instinctively and without thought, for their safety, they ran past a beaming Bob and a bewildered Gary.

Yelling behind her as her feet hit the courtyard she ordered, "Bob, Gary pass the word, no one is to engage the attackers head-on, use shields or try to take them by surprise." Not bothering to see if she was heard, she ran with Hector into a citadel alive with the sounds of death and destruction.

HUNTING KINGS

They found Mira where Bella had left her, in her private parlour. Although no attackers had made themselves known on the way, the screams of the queen's guards were a good indication that the doors needed to be barred and fast.

After the doors were sufficiently barred, Bella felt like a cornered animal, judging by the loud bangs, it would not be long before there was a gaping hole. She was usually good at thinking on her feet. Still, they were trapped, it was not like they could leap out of the window, while affording a good view, the royal apartments overlooked the sea and jagged cliffs. Acting on instinct she pushed Mira into the nearest alcove and pulled a curtain across. Panicked she looked around dumbly for a hiding place of her own. Exasperated by her lack of action Hector shoved her behind a large divan and quickly followed. It was as their eyes met in panic, that the imagined hole in the door, became a reality. Aware of Mira's exposed location on the opposite side of the room, she yelled obscenities at the envisioned attackers to draw their fire. The ploy worked spectacularly, their hiding place peppered with a barrage of heat, force and darkness which pushed them and their once solid divan, towards the cold fireplace behind it. it became quickly evident that their choice of hiding place was a poor one because cloth, fluff and wood went flying everywhere.

Hector brought her back from panic, yelling to be heard above the din, "ANY IDEA'S?" Feeling a momentary sense of fear, because she thought he was asking her to make a decision, she froze.

Luckily, her gaze fell upon the hearth of the fireplace that they had been forced towards only moments before. A dark blast had impacted upon the stone and shining through was a few ancient symbols. The symbols were in a language, with which she was acquainted. They were part of an ancient language Morgan had requested she learn. The knowledge of their meaning caused a thread to appear in her mind, following the thread she found hidden strength, and responded calmly to the fear in Hector's voice, "Yes I do, when I say now, hurl our divan at them." Instead of commenting that their only cover would be gone, he nodded dutifully. Waiting only long enough for another blast, she yelled, "NOW." Already on the move in one swift and precise movement, she reached her hand towards the symbols that spelt, "Hupernikao." As her fingers touched the cold stone beneath, they continued through what should have been solid layers, to grab the object, hidden behind. Turning, she brought the weapon, which she now held to bear, and let it rip. After only a few seconds, she turned to see, a look of awe upon Hector's face. Surprised she set eyes on the object, which she held and then the scene in front of her. A recurve bow unlike any she had ever seen. The white wood glowed in a manner that inferred it was alive and although nought an arrow was nocked, white flaming arrows had simply appeared from an invisible string, as she had released. Her arrows burned where they found a home, leaving only a smouldering pile of what looked to be a tar substance. The arrows themselves disappeared soon after. Standing open mouthed for a second, and despite the strong urge, she did not drop the bow; instead, she placed it gently over her shoulder and went to check on Mira. Hector was so bewildered by what he had just seen; he tripped over a footstool and proceeded to rub the offended limb. It was as she was checking Mira for injuries and Mira, who in turn, was clucking at her burns, that Gary and Bob came steaming into the room yelling a slurry, of panic-induced words. Hector had to use a commanding voice on them before they slowed down, it was Gary that managed to make sense first. "Your Grace, a squad, just rode in from the northern sentry tower they reported seeing a large contingent of those things, riding out towards the North East." He pointed at the piles of tar and then screwed up his nose after realizing where he was indicating.

"Shit." Hector knew why she swore because he went to follow her from the room before they could get very far, Mira called out sternly, "You are hurt, my dear."

"I will survive." She replied briskly, feeling the urge to be moving.

Before she could turn, however, Mira's voice rang out again, this time wavering in fear, "Please, bring my sons home to me."

She met Mira's eye, "I will undertake that task, with every fibre of my being," She said, the conviction of her words propelling her to action.

Hector, Bob and Gary were at her side, and as they strode the long hall, she broke into commander mode and started barking orders, "Gary, get Tallulah out of her kennel and get her and my horse ready for a long ride." Not bothering to respond to her, Gary hurried off to do her bidding, "Bob, have Darren and Randall and a full squad of mounted King's Guard, meet me in the courtyard." Bob response was to, sprint down the hallway.

Hector waited long enough for Bob to leave earshot, then he asked incredulously, "Can you please tell me, what just happened back there?"

Unsure of the words, she did not reply until her feet hit the guest quarters, there she said hesitantly, "I'm positive, you wouldn't believe me if I tried to explain."

Scoffing in response, he said sarcastically "Oh so like I wouldn't believe it, if you told me, you just put your hand through a wall, only to pull out a bow with an imaginary string that shoots endless flaming arrows, which melt people."

Finally making it to her room, she grabbed her pack and bedding roll, feeling silly all she could say in response was, "Good point." Looking up, she beheld a strange expression upon Hector's usually stern face, "What? you have a peculiar look, upon your face?" She asked.

Hector's reply and endearment caused her heart to shudder, "I've only ever seen glimpses of your, all action decisive side. I got to say, I like it."

THE TEMPERATURE HAD DROPPED as the afternoon wore on, an unwelcome reminder that winter was right around the corner. Scanning the countryside for the right spot to call it a night, Leo lamented the meagre haul they had so far and listened to Sha who felt the need to fill the silence as always, with his voice. The small hunting party was reasonably quiet aside from the drone of his brother's voice. Leo didn't mind. He was used to Sha's over-exuberant communication method, he just hadn't dealt with it in a long time, which of course meant, he was still adjusting, even after nearly four weeks of such. Sha had decided to talk for the hundredth time about his family life at Crewtown, "I think this trip has enabled me to get some sleep, even though it's on the ground. The triplets are adorable, don't get me wrong but sleep is a thing of the past, not to mention I don't think Morgan and I have been intimate in, ah, well I can't remember when."

Ignoring his men's uncomfortable glances. Leo felt he was the last person to advise about marriage but gave the reply that was expected, "Why don't you go on a Parentday, you know a parent holiday, you would get a little time alone with Morgan, we are after all nobles, we can do such things."

Sha gave him the look of a scandalized parent then exclaimed incredulously, "But I could never. I'm having enough issues being here with you, the only reason Morgan let me go, was because I promised we would talk about lifting your ban on making more flying ships for commercial purposes."

Thinking better than to point out, that Sha needed permission to leave his home, he felt it didn't matter what he said because Sha's mood would ensure a swift comeback; therefore he brought out his best impression of their mother and said, "You know what they say about couples born out of high-pressure situations, normal life seems boring."

Sha grinned at him, and jovially replied, "Your motherly advice is shit."

Luthor emitted a deep throaty warning which echoed around the clearing. Vapour vented from their horses' nostrils as all in the hunting party halted in unison. Knowing that such a growl meant that something was very close, he gripped his spear tighter in readiness for their prey to come forth. He suddenly found himself wishing for a cornered boar as a sharp cracking of branches heralded a nightmarish sight. Charging out of the bushes and onto the game path before them was twenty robed figures looking decidedly evil. Eyes hidden behind hoods on their black attire, some of the figures seemed to be chanting something under their breaths that Leo could not hear. Worse still, their hands made circular motions in front of them, inside the eerie movements, dark spheres of smouldering energy were growing in size. Sha was the first to act, whacking Hermes rump hard with the flat of his spear the horse got the idea and smartly veered towards the closest bushes to get himself and his master to safety. Fighting an over-whelming urge to turn his horse back towards the night-mare behind him, Leo reminded himself his men needed to concentrate on the fight. A blast hurtled past, singeing his ear simply from proximity, and he heard screams from men and horses alike. The conjured projectiles of darkness that came his way were a good indicator of the attacker's inten-tions, and so he smartly focused all his efforts to stay low in the saddle. The trees around him turned into millions of flying toothpicks as the projectiles met them. It was just as Hermes reached full stride that it happened. A searing sensa-tion flared in his side that seemed to intensify exponentially, looking down in surprise the movement caused waves of pain to threaten unconsciousness. His pristine leather armour now had a sizeable burn hole on the left side. Shaking from the pain it was all he could do to stay on the saddle, but keep on he did, all the while Hermes carried him away from his brother and the men who were risking their lives for him.

It wasn't long before Leo felt himself weaken from the pain, a whistle told Hermes to take him home, and he slumped as best as pain allowed. The effort to keep himself astride took everything he had, every bump causing sharp, sweat beading pain. The night was nearly upon him when his energy finally gave out. The result sudden, he simply wasn't on his saddle any longer, not prepared, when he hit the ground the pain far outweighed preparation, therefore consciousness was lost.

It was the warmth of Luthor sleeping at his uninjured side that he woke to. Teeth gritting together Leo pushed with all his might to get his torso upright, a quick assessment of his predicament brought bleak understanding. A lack of energy and the possibility of walking back to the citadel he hoped that Hermes had made it home so they could send aid. There wasn't much he could do in his injured state any movement caused pain, the worst of which was the melted edges of his armour wearing against the rawness of an open wound. Infection was a possibility; he was recalling what his mother had taught him about burns when Luthor warned of an arrival. The dark figures weren't in a hurry they had their prey, stopping to get off their horses, they gave him their best welcoming sneers, it was as one moved his hands in a familiar fashion, that he realized they had no intention of keeping him alive, closing his eyes to the certainty, he breathed in what he thought was his last breath. A strangled cry caused him to open his eyes again. Luthor had decided that the one who was casting his darkness in his master's direction needed to have two fang marks in his neck. As the caster lay bleeding to death on the ground, another assailant decided Luthor was a more dangerous target and started his dark arts in the new direction. Whistling for Luthor to run home didn't work, instead Luthor came to his side heckles raised, vibrating the ground around them with his growl. Protectively placing his arm around his furry friend, he squeezed with all his might and this time met the evil in front of him with eyes open. Before his enemy's hands did what, he assumed was a release of dark energy, the unsuspecting assailant was impacted by a flaming white arrow. After the arrow burned a hole through his chest, the assailant disappeared, leaving only a black substance and hooded robes. Doing his best to turn in the direction the arrow had originated, he was afforded a beautiful sight. A fierce angel in green Bella rode towards him, her legs controlling the animal beneath, as she fired bright arrows at any that meet her fury. Hector leapt from his saddle and Bella continued to cover as he knelt to check Leo's injuries. With a concerned look on his face, his friend looked to Bella and called, "He's not in a good way, we have to get him back to Bastien, now!"

Although Bella's tone was neutral, there was a distinct edge of concern, in her reply, "Get him home, I need to find Sha."

He was unable to ponder Bella's words, as the act of lifting him upon Hermes saddle brought with it a fight to stay conscious. As Hector made another pass, in his checks to ensure his safety, he reached out and after weakly grasping his friends arm he pleaded, "Go with her."

"My duty is to you, my king." Hector said, not looking up from his task.

Trying to summon strength, he replied, "Then I order you to go."

Hector readjusted the padding that was protecting him from bumps, before replying, "just rest now Leo, I've got you," the sadness in his friends voice was not lost on him. Infuriatingly pain took away worry, soundly replacing it with the gift of darkness.

TALLULAH RACED AHEAD OF HER, Darren and Randall behind. Stopping often, to let her dog find a scent or rest their horses, it was only a few days into the chase that fear threatened to overwhelm. The good news was, they hadn't killed Sha, Bella knew that from the distinctive pattern of Sha's horse's hooves on the ground, his charger trained to take no other rider. The bad news was, they were setting a breakneck pace and had little care for the health of their horses. Worse still, it seemed the direction of the chase was the coast; it was all this information meeting which heralded worry and fear. It seemed apparent to her that the attack on the citadel was simply a diversion. As always, she did not feel up to the task ahead of her. All she could do was continue and hope.

Days slipped by, and the chase wore on, all the while they continued resting dog and horses alike, as much as they dared. Dead horses started to appear on the trail, the depressing sight heightening a worry that only grew with every dead animal. It was as they reached a settlement the apprehension bloomed into frustration and fear of failure, not one villager was spared from the vicious attack and all horses were either killed or used to reach the goal of the coast. She refused to accept what evidence and experience told her. Spurring her tired animal onwards she kept on task.

A little over a day later a blue shimmer informed her that they had reached the coast, exhausted and sick from worry she spurred her horse onwards. As the sight of the sea extended before her an unwelcome sight befall her. Already moving a ship was luffing to get under full sail. In desperation, she kicked her tired horse into the breakers and fired the stark white arrows of her bow. A temporary high of seeing the mainsail envelope into flame, soon dashed by the ship's momentum taking it outside the range of her bow, leaping off her horse she stashed her weapon at her shoulder. Clenching her fists at her sides, she screamed in anguish at the sight of the ship carrying Sha getting smaller on the horizon. Remembering her promise she leapt back onto the saddle, tears streaming, her heart was sore at the thought, of having to report on her failure to Leo, Mira and especially Morgan.

PARENTDAY

Morgan Jones flew The Tempest into Crewtown a conqueror. Despite the small amount of initial resistance, the residing pirates had left with tails between legs. It probably had something to do with the intimidating sight of a hovering ship captained by a hero, spurting flames like a menacing dragon. Despite the chilly air, Morgan stood on her balcony, caught in contemplation as she drank in the view afforded to her. A gust of cold kissed her check, a warning of winter weather to come. Placing her coffee down, she leaned over the balustrade and breathed in the sea air; the smell brought a longing for ship and crew alike. Although the Crewtown she once knew was forever changed, the view before her carried with it pride and contentment. Marlo had commandeered the help of some expert stonemasons, to cut her seat of power into the Crewtown mountainside. The impressive mansion overlooked the town, shipyard and Academy beneath it. The sprawling Academy, as new as it was, already boasted an endless stream of wannabe sailors or flighties. Not only could one learn to man the ropes on one of the kingdoms finest flying ships, but you could also learn field healing, navigation, shipbuilding, and swordsmanship, to name a few. She had sought out the best instructors and still had a few academic gaps. Her old ship could be found at the Academy, now a hands-on learning tool. The dawning day awoke her from reminiscing, spurred onwards by the sounds drifting up from the once quiet town beneath her, she strode inside, where the sight of a messy room greeted her. Although she could afford servants, she hated the idea of someone doing her chores. Her room however, was the only place she afforded mess. When Sha tripped over something it usually prompted him to clean. Therefore, the state of the room brought with it a yearning for Sha's company. Sighing, she walked out into the bowels of the mansion; it was time to check on the other loves of her life.

A very grumpy looking Arlo greeted her as she walked into the nursery. Piper who was helping him waved a hand behind his back, a clear and frantic warning of Arlo's mood. Piper's other hand secured Fareya against her hip; the middle triplet's relaxed demeanour made her the easiest child to handle. Morgan was sure Fareya's smarts would make her the ringleader in any trouble. Trying to defuse Arlo's mood, she smiled her brightest I am a morning person and I'm not ashamed of it smile and said, "Morning Arlo, how are you on this stunning Crewtown day."

Her brightness did not save her from the onslaught, instead it served as a catalyst for Arlo's sarcastic moaning, "It's great you asked actually, now where shall I start. The triplets are teething again. Darwain and Gareth have been crying all night, and I'm sure when they are about to settle Fareya cries simply to start them up again."

Smiling at Arlo, she spoke cooperatively to belay his fears, "Never fear, I've got a few reports to view and despatches to send, then I will come up here and take over so you can get some much-deserved rest." The scathing look Arlo directed towards her was one a mother would use on a child to convey disapproval, although she did not know for sure because her mother never used such. Deciding the best way around was to go straight through, she reiterated, "I promise I will be right back."

Arlo's well-practised look simply deepened, without words this man could convey so much, caving in under the onslaught she acquiesced, "Why don't you bring them into my office, in an hour, that's the best I can do." After an overly exaggerated sigh, Arlo turned back to his work.

Dismissed and in her own home nonetheless, she took the hint and headed for her office.

As she walked the main hallway, she muttered under her breath, lamenting the fact that Sha was having fun with his brother, while she was at home keeping the fires lit and dealing with the nanny. Arlo was usually not so tightly wound, but he was only one man, and the triplets were a special kind of diabolical.

Her office was located below in a quiet corner of the main workshop, her decision to set up in such a random place, was because Marlo's workshop was separate from the bustle of the Academy, but it was still close to the mansion. The way to the workshop was unique, to say the least, forever surprising and especially intelligent, Marlo had designed an original way of reaching it. She had chosen a more apt name, than the one in which Marlo had suggested for his invention. The Ara was powered by one of Marlo's fire chambers; it used stored heat to lift a platform between levels. The word Ara she had borrowed from the tribes-people who lived in the Hanan mountains behind Crewtown. The Mountain Tribes had helped to bring many of Marlo's ideas to life, said ideas were everywhere she looked these days, their lives forever changed by the ease such inventions brought. Leo had decreed that these creations, were not to leave Crewtown until the enemy known as the Master was defeated. The only exception to Leo's decree, was the Crown's order of ships which were being worked on covertly by Marlo and his team of budding shipbuilders.

Morgan walked out into the chilly morning; the ships platform stretched out before her. The Platform hugged the mountainside and boasted the only fleet of flying ships in the Realm. Reaching the Ara, she stepped in and tapped her foot after pulling the desired lever. The workshop was one level below, and beneath that at ground level was the build room and Academy, where ships and students alike were moulded into something more.

She stepped into a workshop alive with energy. Marlo, the queen bee, was at the centre of the room at his drafting desk, mumbling under his breath and occasionally stopping to call out orders to his apprentice Tanner or yell at the odd shipbuilder. Most of the shipbuilders were running between Marlo's workshop and the build room below where the latest ship was coming alive. She called out in welcome and waited patiently for Marlo to look up over the top of his spectacles and notice her. Marlo was viewing the blueprints of his latest invention the Shoreskip, she still had no idea what he was designing, but knowing him, it would be another jewel in his Crown. When Marlo finally looked up, he asked the same question which he greeted her with every morning, "Do we know, if any of my inventions are allowed to leave Crewtown yet?"

Sighing, she said apologetically, "I'm working on it, but it's pretty hard to ignore Leo's reasoning, he doesn't want the enemy to get access to them." Marlo employed his typical, guilt-producing eyebrow raise. she continued in earnest, "Besides, we are behind schedule with the Kings order, we have only got two complete Ascender class ships and another six in production, I have no bargaining chip without a complete order."

An altogether polite clearing of a throat, brought their attention towards Marlo's apprentice who was quietly waiting to speak, "Out with it boy, we haven't got all day." Marlo barked, impatient in his grumpiness.

Tanner was far from a boy, but coming from someone who could live as many years as Marlo, she understood. Tanner was hesitant at first, but their silence gave him confidence, "You could use your Shoreskip prototype, to speed up the production of the ship's, once the upgraded combustion chamber is complete that is."

They both stared at Tanner, Morgan because she had no idea what he was talking about, "Why the-, didn't I think of that." Marlo said, his comment had a well-placed expletive in the middle. Her presence forgotten, Marlo started fiercely scribbling notes at his beach. Arlo and Piper choose that moment to walk in, their arms laden with babies. Piper walked over to Marlo and off loaded Fareya. Marlo interrupted his sudden burst of activity to hold out his arms, eagerly awaiting the impartation of his favourite baby. Free and clearly in a hurry to start her day, Piper pecked her on the cheek and waved goodbye as she exited the room. Despite being only twelve summers, Piper liked to pass her time by helping out around the Academy. By all accounts, Piper's help was appreciated, it wasn't just her nature that people enjoyed, she was a sponge for knowledge, of which the instructors were more than happy to impart. Often, to her joy, Piper came home from a day of work exuberantly spouting a new piece of animated information. Busy at his work Marlo continued to hold Fareya in one arm, quill in the opposite hand. Before long Marlo's inkpot was knocked over due to his lack of equilibrium, oblivious to the child, he swore. Fareya, who was very good at parroting those around her, repeated Marlo's swearword perfectly. Smartly deciding it was an excellent time to exit, before Arlo and Marlo griped at each other, she accepted Fareya from a guilty-looking Marlo and walked into her office. Her office was her favourite place outside of her day room. Gently settling Fareya on the ground she sat on the floor and waited for Arlo to place Gareth and Darwain, before leaving and covertly peeking around the corner to ensure that Arlo wasn't loitering. When the coast was clear she started her morning exercises, all the while talking to her children to keep them amused, "Mummy has the world on her shoulders darlings, and I can't stop now, you understand don't you." Her children who were used to her verbal musings, got the idea very quickly and when she stretched into a bridge position they made their move. Gareth was the first to climb aboard with a giggle, not one to follow Fareya decided that it was a better idea to crawl beneath her and look up with a lopsided smile, Darwain leaned against her adding his weight to the mix. Continuing under the added strain, she decided to make it a little harder, "You are all coming on a ride to destiny," she said, bending her arms into a push up. Reaching the bottom of a push-up, she imparted a kiss, upon a giggling Fareya's forehead.

She had just put an arm behind her back for added difficultly, when a stern comment startled her, "Seriously, Morgan, this brings a new low, to multitasking."

Standing over her with crossed arms, tapping his foot and looking disapproving, was Arlo. Deciding that she had better stand up for herself or she would find her captainship stolen out from underneath her, she growled her response, "I love this newfound ability to express yourself Arlo, but you are skating on thin ice. To put it mildly, if you were on my ship you would be thirty shades of purple, and if you didn't scare away every other nanny, you would have more help!"

Arlo swallowed, looking rather castigated, he expertly grabbed all three children using only two arms, apparently in a rush to rescue them from their suddenly grumpy mother. Sighing and with a mind that wouldn't stop, she pushed up with her arms and legs and grabbed her quarterstaff. Her staff was now her preferred weapon. Slipping into a comfortable rhythm, she sent the staff out and back, flicking and spinning, quickly feeling more focused. After her exertions she stopped to write letters and read reports, it was when she was feeling like her day was finally on track, that she heard a commotion coming from the workshop. Because her office was devoid of a door, she was gifted with a maddening commotion that included a lot of giggling and wistful sighing noises. Such noises were not allowed in Marlo's workshop unless Marlo had visited the Rose & Tickle and had decided to work on some idea his drinking session had triggered. Not that much had ever come of such. Leaning back on her chair she took a sneak peek around the corner to glean the source of the commotion, the result of which was her falling backwards, taking her chair with her in surprise. There in Marlo's workshop was none other than Castain and Aiden, she hadn't seen either in over two years, yet they seemed to be picking up where they had left things. Castain stood with his arms crossed, watching the scene before him. Aiden was surrounded in what Morgan could only describe as groupies. Four of her woman crewmembers riveted by Aiden's every word, his horrible joke about Arlo's new name being Manny, meaning man nanny, seemed to set them off like a pack of dolphins; their high-pitched glee grating on her ears. Meena stood in a similar stance to Castain, the subtle difference being that her eyes rolled every time Aiden finished a sentence.

FIRST ABOVE ALL

*P*icking herself up off the floor, Morgan dusted off her pants and pulled her shirt edge down to what she hoped was straighter. Seeing Castain, gave her an uninvited feeling of nervous apprehension as if a rogue wave was coming and she needed to brace for impact.

She did not announce her presence instead she quietly took up a position across from Castain and beside Meena. Castain's only indication that he saw her, a slight inclination of the head. Crossing her arms, she stood watching the exchange before her, Aiden's handsome face animated amidst his tale, he held his groupies in awe, "I nearly died, if it wasn't for my trusty horse I am certain I would be dead." His story, absurdly unlikely, she stood amused, anticipating the outcome, "My horse Prancer, was the real hero, thank goodness we managed to hoist him aboard."

It was at that point that Aiden was interrupted by a highly amused Meena who decided not to let his comment pass, "Your horse's name is Prancer!" Meena blurted, clutching her sides she walked from the room unable to contain her laughter. Watching her friend's rare display of mirth, she looked back and was surprised to see a distinct look of yearning upon Aiden's face, his eyes following Meena's exit.

Brady, who seemed to be in the running for the job of head groupie, was hanging onto Aiden's every word, with a husky lilt to her voice, she said, "And then what happened?" As if inspecting his bicep she casually moved her hand down his arm; consequently, Aiden let out a squeal of surprise.

Not one to bow out when a challenge was afoot, Taymah casually leaned in from Aiden's other side, staring at his lips with a smouldering pout, she purred seductively into his ear, "Actuals, oh you poor, poor man." Although Morgan could not see it from her angle, a hand must have grabbed Aiden's behind, as when the word, "Man" was uttered, he leapt straight into the air, hand covering behind, and let out another undignified squeal. Aiden was apparently used to a different type of woman, like a lamb to the slaughter, his voice was increasing an octave, as he continued to speak. Deciding that it was time to come to Aiden's rescue before she had a catfight on her hands Morgan cleared her throat loudly, consequently, the groupies all found sudden excuses to leave and go about their business. A look of sheer gratitude met Aiden's features, and when he spoke, as always his manners were impeccable bowing at the precise level he said, "As always a pleasure your ladyship, it's nice to see your beautiful face."

Involuntarily snorting at his comment, she quickly composed herself. However, Marlo's grin threatened to re-topple propriety, replying in kind she joined warmly, "We do not stand on formality here Aiden. Unless you are on my ship, you are welcome to address me as a friend or as an equal."

Aiden's dimpled smile was well-practised, she got the impression that he thought he was charming, "I guess you are wondering why we have graced you with our presence after so long." He said cordially.

"Yes, I was wondering that, will you please fill me in," She said harshly, already impatient with the pretence.

Castain did not waste words so she was not surprised by his silence. Aiden continued, his love of attention evident in the way he held himself, "The reason we have come here first, instead of Bastien, is because amidst all the intel we have heard some very troubling news, mostly affecting you." At her nod Aiden continued, "Not only are there reports that the enemy is amassing large quantities of dragons fire, but also we have had word that they plan to steal a flying ship to reverse engineer Marlo's design."

Marlo interrupted, his response sceptical and lengthy, "Well that's just impossible this is the most heavily fortified port in the kingdom, we have cannons on the cliffs, cannons suspended on wires over the harbour, yes, you heard me right. Not to mention there is no other way to arrive unless you go through a gauntlet of towers in the harbour," Marlo stopped to take a breath then continued, "Which are armoured with, you guessed it, more cannons. Don't even get me started on the armament aboard the ships, which are ready to back up any attack, at a moment's notice, it is impossible!"

Raising her eyebrow's at Marlo in a manner that implied there was no such thing as impossible. She addressed Aiden her tone leaving no room for dissent, "I thank you for this information, we will do a full sweep of all fortifications to see what we can find, in the meantime I will arrange some rooms at the Rose & Tickle and show you around, just let me finish a despatch."

Marlo, who was looking at her grumpily, suddenly changed his tune, despite the newness of the day he was always happy at the prospect of visiting his favourite watering hole and thought to invite himself.

Thoughts already on other tasks, she turned to head in the direction of her office. She was waylaid by a very determined-looking Castain, who although had nothing to say thus far, choose that moment to plant himself in front of her. Castain had an intense stare yet his words were delivered gently, "I would say, judging from your demeanour that you haven't read my letter."

Castain's remark took her by surprise, she stammered in reply, "ah, um, oh, ah sorry I have been a little busy, but I will go read it now." Inclining his head respectfully, Castain politely moved aside, then joined the discussion that Marlo and Aiden were having about the merits of letting one's inventions see the light of day.

Left bracing for the wave that was upon her, Morgan walked back into her office. It was where it had always been, hidden at the bottom of her writing box, deliberately overlooked, red wax seal unbroken, a pile of old opened letters placed on top. Lifting the pile, she retrieved the letter Castain had written over two years earlier, and as if fragile she gently placed it on the desk in front of her. Knowing that, what it said could bring so much change, and afraid that reading the words could bring a reality she wasn't sure she was ready for; therefore she continued looking at it in apprehension. Gazing absently, she reached her hand out to close the letter-box. It did not take her long to feel silly, and so deciding the best approach was to rip off the bandage. She swore at herself and lifted the letter, flicking the wax seal with the dagger she kept handy, her brain threatened to freeze. It was too late now; momentum was afoot, she opened a door in her life that brought such a wide array of feelings to her senses, that none could win in their battle to compete for her attention.

. . .

DEAR MORGAN,

I am writing this letter, after once again being sent on a mission for the crown. I wanted to wait for you to wake, to talk of this, but it wasn't meant to be. You gave me a distinct impression you already know; however, I will write the words, I am your father.

Watching you over the last month has left me without a doubt that you are a piece of me, a part of my reason for being, my will, and not to mention all the other things I have hidden, to keep you safe since you were born. Not a day goes by that I don't think of you. I have kept a constant watch on you all these years and regret that I was not there on the day the Dragon was taken. I am proud of your strength as a leader, and the ability to command your crew with decisiveness even at sixteen years old.

I can imagine you think I am abandoning you again, but my duty to my king has always been a part of who I am. I hope someday you come to understand that I never wanted to leave you. The pain and sadness of failure and guilt cannot be quenched. My duty as always, comes first above all, even before anything I desire. I will not write about the importance of duty, that is not fair. One day, I hope you will come to understand that, I did what I did, for you.

In awe of you, your father
Reginald Cuisenaire the Third, Earl of Hautbas

WIPING AT THE TEARS, that had unceremoniously decided to fall, it took a few moments for her to realise that she was shaking. So many emotions crashed into her head. Over-whelmed, she hated the sudden lack of control, all because of a man who dared give himself the title of father. Using the only option available she reacted, striding into Marlo's work-shop, she opened flood gates of emotion that were hidden, where they rightly belonged. Only barely aware Arlo had brought her children in to visit, her onslaught of words struck out, as if a verbal assault in Castain's direction, "Why, why would you do this, why couldn't you just say these words to my face, first above all, who the heck says that shit!"

With anger that mirrored her own, Castain's reply was gruff, although there was a sadness behind his eyes, "I tried, you shut me down twice, you knew what was in that letter, don't pretend you didn't."

She paid no head, her anger palpable in the shaking of her fists, one of which held the crumpled letter, it was while she was ignoring Castain's words, that she noticed Arlo and the young visitors. Letting out a frustrated grunt in a concerted effort to distance her fury from her children, she turned and headed back to her office, "Holy shit, are you kidding me, who says this in a letter!" She screamed in frustration.

The distinct tiny voice of Fareya could be heard in the new silence of the workshop, "shit."

Furious, she continued to vent, "Argh, I need a door to this office." The fact, said door would have been slammed, made her feel like a child having a tantrum and listening to the hastened noises of Arlo exiting, in a hurry to get her children away from their tyrant of a mother, guilt added to competing emotions.

Feeling guilt, anger sadness and even a tinge of happiness, the breath she was holding in was released, when Marlo's voice cut an awkward air, "Ok lads, follow me to the Rose & Tickle, first drinks on me."

Sinking into her chair, she waited for the workshop to empty, before forcefully flinging throwing knives towards a target, all the while longing for the uplifting, supportive presence of her husband.

Days of self-enforced duty followed, and as the adult, Morgan thought she was, she tried to work through her emotions. Yet her mind was at war, said war caused her to long for the Tempest of old, a rolling sea and her rum fuelled rollicking crew amidst a round of Captains Bastard. She was acutely aware that keeping herself deliberately busy was an attempt to regain control. Still, she didn't care, which is how she found herself wasting her afternoon, listening to a self-important instructor prattle on about the issues he was having with a lack of resources, namely feathers for quills. I mean really, it wasn't like he couldn't get off his arse and get some. Nodding dumbly, she berated herself for her lack of attention, it was as she was mentally slapping herself in the face, that she noticed one of her runners speed up. The boy had clearly made an effort to make haste, the sweat and puff an indicator of such. As he sucked in air, she patiently waited for him to get his breath back when a panicked message finally came out of the boy, his words took her by surprise, "Your Ladyship, The Fancier, has sent for you, a red-letter has come from Bastien, it's in your office." Suddenly she was in a state of heightened awareness, a red-letter was a term for royal mail at the highest level of importance, usually around war, death or births.

Not looking back and without a word, she hurried away from the instructor who was mid-sentence, as she rushed through the workshop on the way to her office, the omen of Castain, Aiden, Meena, Piper and Arlo waiting expectantly as if a council of support, was concerning. The council's demeanour coupled with the grave looks upon their faces gave her stomach a sharp dip. Clearly Aiden had received correspondence of his own. Hastening to her desk as fast as her legs could carry her, she picked up the letter. Remembering the last time she had read a letter at her desk, she froze, an internal voice soothed, *"it can't be as bad, as the last one."* Another thought quickly followed, *"be careful, what you wish for."* As she had already started to read, her eyes locked on the words before her.

. . .

DEAR MORGAN,

I WRITE to you in great haste,

SHA HAS BEEN KIDNAPPED. I am so sorry, I have failed you. I won't give you too much detail because I know that you will want to get moving. It has taken me nearly three weeks to get back to the citadel after the pursuit of the kidnappers. We were attacked by what we are now calling Dark Acolytes, too late, did we discern the real target was Sha and Leo. I'm so sorry I didn't get to him in time, please make all haste to Astrom. A fisherman has relayed that he sighted the ship heading on that bearing.

WITH ALL WRETCHEDNESS, your Friend Bella.

PS PLEASE BE CAREFUL, The Dark Acolytes have what I can only assume is magic.

IT WAS TOO MUCH; her brain went into full meltdown. No movement, no sound, even thoughts froze in her shocked mind. White knuckles gripped either side of her writing desk. She ignored Castain's concerned statement about her wellbeing as he walked in, his attempts to get her attention disregarded. Words did not reach her.

Castain must have been there long enough to get frustrated, because she instinctively grabbed the piece of wood thrown at her head. In her hands, her trusty staff, there was no time to ponder as she had to raise the staff to block a blow aimed at the side of her head. Castain had picked up her practise staff and decided to try to jolt her into action. Apparently, Castain thought being a parent meant aiming a forceful blow at one's head. Castain's act was enough to bump her readily available and fresh anger to the surface. Finally, an emotion she could use, and so she used it, pushing Castain back with strikes and sweeps, flicking and twisting in all her fury. When Castain spoke it was to lecture, "What are you doing! are you a cowardly merchant, or a fearless pirate! You need to move! NOW."

Her reply streamed from the honesty she had wanted to employ after reading his letter, "You ask what I am, I? I will tell you, I am what I made myself with no help from you. You don't get to come in this late in the piece and tell me how to live my life."

She aimed a sweep at Castain's legs, in response he deftly flipped backwards like an acrobat. They had somehow made it into the larger workshop area, and they were putting the space to good use. Locked in a battle of wills she quickly found herself impressed even hard-pressed with the opponent before her. As if Castain could read her very thoughts he seemed to be answering her strikes with his own. Aiden, clearly stunned by the view in front of him, said to Meena, "Have you ever seen such a display of skill, by one person, let alone two? Do you think this is how they will settle family disagreements?"

Ignoring the comment, she put all her efforts into reaching Castain with her staff; nothing worked, desperation brought chaos to her strikes. She did not like the lack of control he brought into her life, and now he dared to stop her from letting her staff meet the side of his head. Castain's lecture continued, "Why aren't you moving, you know it's the right decision, I can't imagine you would trust, anyone else to rescue him."

Letting him have it with a spinning mid swipe then stepping on the back foot to guard against his attacks, she employed honesty, deflating with every word she spoke, "Of course I want to go, I love him with every fibre of my being. Not that you would understand this but I must think of my children, what if we don't come back they will be parentless, just like me."

Her last words echoed around the workshop. She went on the defensive Castain's words had broken through her façade, "You are not parentless, nor have you ever been one to brood, now get off your arse and move." Castain's comment proceeded by a lightning-fast sweep which took her off her feet, and she found herself on the aforementioned body part.

Normally she would have leapt back onto her feet, but she was empty. Castain stood over her holding out his hand, his words calming the storm, "I will make sure you come back you may not want me for a father, but I know you as I know myself, together we will make them pay."

Arlo was the next to speak, "Don't worry about the triplets, I will look after them," grudgingly he continued, "I will even try to get along with the other nannies. That is if they don't piss me off too much."

She grabbed Castain's hand, allowing him to help her up, all the while yelling for a runner. The boy that entered the room looked up at her shyly, bending down to his level, she announced, "Round up my crew the ship leaves at sunrise." Nodding, the runner went about his task. Looking around, she asked, "Where is Marlo?"

Before she heard, Arlo's response, she knew the answer, "The Rose & Tickle."

MY DRINKING CREW HAS A
PIRATE PROBLEM

*H*er feet moved with purpose towards The Rose & Tickle, the most pressing errand; not counting down the exact time in hours, minutes and seconds till the ship departed. Morgan would have been happy to leave, but a trip as far as Sirillia meant supplies, not to mention, going unprepared would do Sha no favours. Her thoughts produced an audible sigh, and it was as her hand touched the rough grain of the solid wooden entry, that Aroon purposefully strode up to her, his tall wiry frame and worn face set with a determination that mirrored her own. Knowing she would not take offence, Aroon got straight to the point, "This time, you are not leaving me behind." She did not rebuke him, she knew from growing up in Crewtown what it meant to be a sea dog, being left behind was similar to being put out to pasture. It was separation from that which sustained you, the sea, the air, and the camaraderie of the crew.

"I wouldn't dream of it, although I might need your help in there," Morgan replied tentatively; because she knew what she was asking.

Aroon held the door open then waited patiently for her to step through. It wasn't a gesture because he felt sorry for her, despite a dubious background he was a gentleman. Aroon, like most of her crew, had not let life define who he was.

As she walked over the threshold, the familiar yet random perfume, and yeast aroma of The Rose & Tickle greeted her. For a drinking establishment it was the most pretentious she knew of, the sign on the wall which read 'If you smell, either pay for a bath or drink elsewhere!' was an example of such. Rena's girls were working the room, clad in outfits which clung in a typically scandalous way. Rena had taken her instructions with regards to converting the brothel into a tavern, and executed it in a petulant manner, even the name Rose & Tickle was deliberately selected to scandalise. Little did Rena know, let alone understand, Morgan's request was not about hampering her income or because she disapproved of Rena's business exploits, it was to give the girls options, and to fill a niche in the market, that her academy had created. Although it never bothered her, Rena had yet to admit she had made a small fortune from Morgan's ideas. Rena also had a way of aggravating her tenants; as a result, Morgan had given a lot of her time over to solving disputes, usually with some disgruntled instructor or student. Her eyes scanned the room for Marlo; unsurprisingly, she found him sitting at his favourite spot at the main taproom bar. Marlo was prattling away to an old sailor who sat beside him; the sailor was slumped over the bar sound asleep, quite an impressive feat as he still held his tankard amidst loud snoring which intermittently woke him. Although she was in a hurry, she held herself in check, running around now when she could go nowhere served no purpose. It was, also best to get the lay of the land before interrupting one of Marlo's rants, especially when she desperately needed him at her side. The conversation was one-sided, Marlo's companion was silent aside from the odd grunt. It took her a second to understand that Marlo was slurring a lament on his relationship with alcohol, "Meh an ourcohol, wee need to tak." Marlo burped before and after every comment, "Wee dn't know each otha anymor, naw weally, wee ar groin apart." Slamming his hand down on the counter Marlo continued, the slur of his words making him hard to understand. "Wee nead ta spen mor qualty time geather, so wee re hapy n each otha's compny."

Feeling like she needed to interrupt the unsavoury conversation as it was going nowhere, she said, "Marlo, I don't think that's what you need at all, an unhealthy relationship with alcohol!" She sat next to Marlo and let him take her in with blurry eyes, Aroon casually stood behind. Aware she was deliberately trying to ignore her own gaping issues, she demanded, "Ok out with it, get it off your chest, the ship leaves in the morning, so I need you ready."

As if he was oblivious to her words, after executing the longest beer smelling burp she had ever heard, Marlo started to list his woes, "I hvnt ad a neew idear in months. Me aprentise s brillyant, he keep s showng me yup. Me ventions re stuk yin Crewtown."

Marlo took a swig and looked to add to his rant, like a fish out of the water he opened and closed his mouth. When she was sure nothing was coming forth, Morgan spoke the words she knew Marlo wanted to say, "And, your seemingly adopted daughter has learnt she has a father. You are worried you will lose her and she will forget all the support you have provided her all these years," An increased slump of Marlo's shoulders, was confirmation she had nailed it.

Before she could placate Marlo, the old sailor beside him suddenly straightened in his chair and announced, "A sailor's life is tough, you do back-breaking work all day and night, and you never have any time for family." Although Marlo's drinking friend had already slumped back onto the bar, Marlo replied matter-of-factly, "Shev, ya don woak caus ya own sa many boats an ya don hav eny family."

Continuing astutely aware that she was still ignoring her issues, she decided tough love was in order. Placing her hands firmly on Marlo's tankard she spoke harshly, "Snap out of it, at least you didn't just have it confirmed that your long-lost father Is none other than Reginald-."

Her lecture disguised as a vent was rudely interrupted when Marlo exclaimed, "Wait, did yea say, the ship wa leavin in the morn, 'was going on?"

The comment took her by surprise. Suddenly she found herself having to utter the words out loud, and there was no one more challenging to do that too, than Marlo. her voice rebelled and gave away underlying emotion in an unintended shaky tone, "Sha has been kidnapped, we leave at first light."

Before she could continue, Marlo shot up straight as an arrow then bellowed with surprising clarity, "OH HECK, NO!" It was as Marlo's legs made it to a straight position that he lost all momentum and proceeded to fall towards the ground, his size and weight subsequently produced a loud thud that brought a scowl laden Rena from her office.

Turning to Aroon, she pointed at the heap that was Marlo and said, "That there is what I needed you for."

Aroon sceptically looked at the mass on the ground and grumbled, "I'm going to need some help."

"I got this," Shev announced, shooting out of his seat with a surprising steady countenance. After seeing the surprised looks on their faces, he continued, "What, I just come here for the conversation and sleep."

Well-wishers lined the platform. Even under such sombre circumstances and despite the newness of the sun, it was still a spectacle to watch one of the new ship's leave. Ignoring fatigue caused by a lack of sleep, Morgan forced a smile and stepped up to Piper, placing a hand on her shoulder, she said, "I don't want you to worry, I will find your brother. You are going to have to make the trip back to Bastien without me. I have organised a passage for you, a few days from now."

Piper was coming around to the reality that she was a princess, and despite her new family and life at The Citadel she still insisted on extended visits to Crewtown. Before the current circumstance, Morgan had foreseen the possibility of Piper's life starting to normalise; now she detected worry under the surface. Readily available pout present, Piper replied, "Please don't worry about me at a time like this, are you sure you don't want me to stay here longer, at the least to help look after the triplets?"

"Mira needs you right now. Tell her I will bring him home," She said impassively, amidst the turmoil.

Nodding the once carefree child, said intuitively, "You don't need to make me feel better, just please be careful."

After one of Piper's typical chest squashing hugs she moved on with purpose, stepping up to Arlo and the other nannies, she held each babe in turn. She gently placed a kiss upon their heads, momentarily comforted at the thought that they did not understand her sadness, only to have Fareya cling to her as if reading her underlying anxiety. Nodding to no one in particular, she turned to walk up the gangplank, her feet hitting the wood caused a comforting alignment. No longer a worried wife or messed up child, she was the focused captain of an Ascender class ship, on a mission of utmost importance. Walking straighter, she made her way towards the quarterdeck; it was time.

IT WAS a great surprise to Bella that she had been allowed to sit at Leo's bedside. In a constant vigil, she helped in any way that Mira had allowed. As the days passed, Leo's condition gradually worsened. Bella was in awe of Mira's strength, despite delirium and screams of pain, Mira was steadfast, only allowing her to take over when exhaustion allowed. Like his fever, a sense of uselessness had grown inside of her. Left an emotionless shell, driven onwards only by an underlying stubbornness which her stepmom had tried to beat out of her every chance she had got. Hope lifted in her heart when his fever finally broke despite the fact, he still seemed to be making little sense or had yet to gain consciousness. Coming out of her thought induced daze, she looked up to see Mira was about to give Leo some water. Reaching to help a servant prop him up, Bella dutifully waited for Mira to carefully dribble a small amount into his mouth, again reminded by the weakness of a man that generally exuded strength, and at times even gave her such. She felt a tear escape down her cheek, Mira politely chose not to notice, and it was as she was carefully resettling him on the pillows, that his eyes finally opened. Light blue's fixated upon her, instantly exuding a tenderness that took her breath away. Looking up at Mira, she saw her excitement mirrored there. Caught by their untethered force, feelings that his gaze carried to the surface caused her to freeze. At first, when Leo spoke, his words were croaky, on an unused throat, "Sha, where is Sha?"

She could not reply her tongue held by her failure, only her tears answered him, it was Mira that replied, "He is alive, Lady Ysabella chased the kidnappers to the coast where they managed to escape, Morgan has been told, she will be leaving as we speak."

Leo's face hardened in annoyance; she turned away. She readied herself to be cast aside in all her uselessness. Leo's large hand grip her arm, his voice warm and caring, "I know you well enough to know, you did everything you could." She looked at him in surprise, Leo continued, his words brought vulnerability, "Bell why even now, can't you believe me when I say, I could not, nor will I ever, cast you aside."

Leo's comment was uttered in front of Mira, causing panic yet when she looked up, she saw an unsurprised almost resigned expression upon Mira's face. "Please don't, exert yourself, Leo. I think Mira would agree with me when I say I let Sha fall into the enemy's hands," She said, aware that it was an effect to protect herself.

His hand squeezed her arm, resolute in his words, "Don't do this, this isn't about not being able to rescue Sha, this is about you, thinking you are not worthy."

Mira spoke, her matter-of-fact words shook Bella's equilibrium, as she was backing up Leo's craziness, "That weapon you wield is one of legend. Such a weapon was not given to just anyone."

It was too much, her plan to leave was made up during Leo's fever-induced stupor, but now with only words, he seemed to be changing them again. Deciding she wasn't taking him down with her, she employed honesty and said pointedly, "You know my past Leo."

Leo's answer was typical and broke through all remaining barriers, "Yes, and I am grateful, as your past has made you who you are, from the hidden strength you hide from the world to the gentle kindness you exude. Please believe me when I say as soon as I met you, I thank Amare every day for bringing you into my life, no other could compare, who you are is my love."

The tears were back sweeping decorum aside, not at all helped when Leo grabbed her chin in his big hands and claimed a kiss despite the austere onlooker. Feeling altogether out of sorts, she hastily excused herself. She stopped in the adjoining room to catch her breath, which happened to be when she overheard Leo say, "Mother, I am announcing my engagement as of today."

Mira's reply, caused a sudden bout of hyperventilation, "So be it, son. Bella has proven her worth, I will stand with you, if the court disagrees, hell hath no fury." She was overwhelmed, leaning on the nearest wall for support, her thoughts were erratic, it was all wrong, ready to be cast out one second, accepted the next. Absently feeling around for the nearest chair, she decided it prudent to sit down.

ASCENDING DRAGON

It fell, as soon as foot hit deck. Gentle at first, then more persistent, Morgan's cheeks although protected from the rain by her hat were stung by the chill morning air. She was not bothered, winters timely arrival suited her mood. As she ascended the stairs that led to the quarterdeck, she took in the shiny new ship before her. The triple hull design of the Ascender class was an advancement in every way, most of the improvements were about updating the original design for prolonged flight, speed, and manoeuvrability. She envisaged The Tempest now looked like a shiny white scaled dragon. Dragons were figments of a child's Imagination, based on stories a parent might tell to encourage them towards the bed. Even so, Marlo's flamboyant way of executing his ideas brought imagination to life, discovering a new facet of her ship regularly took her breath away. Aside from the salty air and sway, the only thing she missed about her old ship was hiding from the worst of the cold winter months, spending one's ill-gotten or in her case gotten gain's. Glad for a wax-coated fur-lined jacket, she stood at the top of the stairs taking in the activity. Her eyes stopped on the massive cylindrical metal mast tube which sat where a mainmast would have been on a seafaring ship. Marlo had engineered a special lightweight, white-hued steel, that allowed for equal parts strength and flexibility in the areas of the ship that required such. The same steel was similarly used in the twin aft mast tubes. The aft tubes which jutted outward from the stern gave the ship direction and were scalloped in a way that caused them to flare based on the wheels turn. Positioned higher than the previous tubes, they also allowed for ease of landing on a body of water.

Keeping her face passive, Morgan nodded in Cheese's direction, in response he brought a boatswain's pipe to his lips. The effect of the shrill call caused every crewmember to stare in her direction, she did not falter. Standing in typical stance, legs square and shoulder-length apart, she picked a crew member to look toward and started her pre-lift away speech. Solid and unwavering her voice rang out over the masses, "As you know, we are bound for the continent of Sirillia, a territory full of danger and our enemies. What you may not know, is we go on a rescue mission. Asharn Robert Dallinger, the Baron of Crewtown and my husband, has been kidnapped." Stopping long enough to allow her words to sink in and the din to quieten she continued amidst inner turmoil, "As the protector of the realm I am aware that the mantle does not rest solely upon my shoulders, it also rests upon yours. What does this mean for you?" Pausing, she gathered her breath and continued loudly in a way that sent her voice out forcefully, into the cold morning, "I always say at the start of every voyage, a sword in a scabbard is safe but that is not what they are meant for. On this voyage, our swords must be sharper, stronger, and more precise than they have ever been before. This will be dangerous, this will be hard, some of us may fall, but now like always we will not run from a fight. Sha has never just been our liege, lord, friend, or husband, he exemplifies our hope in a better future. I will fight and if need be die, to go to his aid. You, however have a choice, you can stay or you can go now without condemnation or shame. Now go and find your officers or get off my ship." Her crews deafening reply, echoed off the mountains with a finality that comforted, "Aye, Captain."

The deck became a mass of bodies going about their business. Gruth stood dutifully beside her, Morgan ensured she had his attention before commanding, "Wait five, then give the call to harness, and lift away." Nodding dutifully, Gruth went about his business.

Before long the ship was rising above all but Morgan's underlying fears. The rain was falling onto the aft mast tubes; the resulting vapour produced a menacing effect that quite rightly suited her mood, one hand absently gripping her sheaved cutlass, she left Gruth to duty and went to inspect her ship. Marlo's disgruntled features greeted her on the main deck, he was swaying in place as if missing non-existent waves, one of his large hands gripping the thick starboard aft cable as if it was keeping him upright. One of four thick woven ropes, the cable's connected the ships main anchor points to the expansive gas pocket. Layers of double stitched sailcloth contained the gas pocket, and it was protected by tiered metal tiles that moved and flexed with the pocket. Softening her expression in solidarity, she asked, "I see you are up, how's your head, second?"

Marlo's pale features did not match an overtly stern reply, "Why do you insist, upon calling me that, with your new title the correct rank is number one, or first lieutenant."

Raising her eyebrow in deference to his berating tone, she said playfully, "Because my friend, fear of heights and hangover be damned, you will always be my second."

Looking unsure, Marlo seemed to ponder for a moment, that or he was concentrating on keeping his stomach contents in place. When he finally spoke, it was with a more thoughtful air, "taking into account why we are here right now you don't need to pretend around me or try to make me feel better. I'm fine, but did you have to place me in my cabin, if I had more warning, than that of waking up on a ship lifting into the sky, I would have taken so many things."

"I know, that's why I got your brilliant apprentice to deck out the ship with everything you could need," She replied cheerfully, wholly aware of the inflammatory nature of her words. Marlo groaned in response and walked away, all the while holding his head as if he could keep a splitting headache at bay. The movement was a bad idea, after executing a sudden one-eighty it became clear what Marlo had eaten the night before, because of the manner in which it brutally exited from him.

Frowning at the mess down the side of her shiny new ship, said frown deepened, when Castain spoke cordially from beside her, "What's his problem?"

Her reply was accurate but also much to her surprise, slightly impetuous, "He forgets sometimes that this is a flying ship."

Nodding as if her answer was in fact acceptable, Castain said, "I need a moment of your time." Castain's respectful tone brought uninvited feelings and anger hovered at the edge of her mind. Luckily for Castain they stood aboard The Tempest, a place where command left no room for feelings. Seeing her decisive nod, Castain continued in a typically abrupt manner, "I noticed you have no master at arms, I like to keep myself busy and would like to offer myself for the position."

Castain's unexpected comment forced the air from her lungs, altogether grateful she replied favourably. "With my increased crew numbers, I would appreciate the help, you can start by drilling the boarders." Without hesitation,

Castain left to find the crew that made up her main boarding party. She turned back to re-engage her uplifting and diverting banter with Marlo, only to find him gone. As her crew now had the ability to harness themselves to numerous reinforced anchor points, located wherever one might need such, she called out for a crew member to clean the side of her ship. Pushed by a sudden awareness of lurking thoughts, she headed purposefully into the bowels of the ship in search of a diversion. There she was welcomed by the Tempest's expansive insides. The new ship housed one generous captain's cabin, ten officers' cabins, bunk rooms for over two hundred crew, and lastly the triple hull design with no requirement for spare masts and sails allowed for increased space. Marlo's particular kind of hoarding, however, still took up a lot of room. Thinking about him brought a twinge of guilt, so she decided to go and find if he needed help. Unfortunately for her frayed nerves, when she got to the workshop, she was greeted with the sight of Marlo and Tanner bemusedly staring at an unlikely helper. Looking far from aged, lifting boxes with ease and moving heavy metal sheets, was none other than Marlo's Rose & Tickle drinking buddy, Shev. Astounded, she growled, "Marlo, what the heck is he doing on my ship and why are you just standing there, aren't you worried he will injure himself?"

Marlo's reply was snarky as the decibels in her voice, paid no respect to his hangover, "I have no idea, we found him like this." Opening and closing her mouth for a few seconds, she eventually decided it best to leave, before she said something inappropriate or deployed further ageism. A distinct impression that there were forces at work that she had no control over, played on her already frayed nerves.

· · ·

SWEEP, step, kick, ground, extend, ahh yes there was nothing like it, the precise, decisive movements of unarmed combat, Meena liked to calm her nerves by envisaging her enemies going down, which usually involved bones crushing and blood spraying. She was calm amidst her movements, when a certain tan haired grey-eyed, full of his importance, male, encroached upon her new practise area. She had chosen the lower hold for such because being on deck required one to have a harness and she wasn't a fan of the constriction while practising, that and it was until this moment a good place to hide oneself from the world. Aiden looked ghostly white, and his comment was absurd even for him, "Oh sorry, I'm just a bit seasick, who would have thought on a flying ship, right!" Sighing loudly, she continued as if his absurdity was in fact elsewhere. Then because his arrogance must have been telling him she wanted to speak with him, he dared to continue, "Wow, your movements have greatly improved, when I'm not feeling sick, I would like to spar with you."

As if he wasn't aware of the insult his presence brought, she huffed, yet before leaving the hold, she made sure to get in the last word, "If you were as smart as you say you are, you would know that you would feel less sick at the point of least pivot, which is the deck." Leaving Aiden and the sudden surprised look on his face behind her, she felt an annoying pang of guilt, luckily her feet quickly took her away from the situation and the guilt.

MIRROR OPPOSITES

Morgan's first act was to call her officers to a strategy meeting. Aiden was particularly favourable to the idea, the youngest Spymaster ever at only twenty-five years, it was meticulous planning and organisation that made him what he was. The auspicious location surprised him, the wardroom in the original Tempest, had been used for training. Morgan's motives became apparent in the new faces around him; a larger ship meant more ranked roles among the crew. He loved the idea of a meeting room for the higher echelon, especially now that he needed to avoid what everyone was calling his groupies. The room was noisy until Morgan made her entrance, her very presence triggering hush to spread. He was unsure if this was because of the clear respect she merited or because they all felt sorry for her. Either way, he politely sat back and waited for the meeting to start. Possibly to channel the energy away from her, Morgan skipped all formalities and began the discussions at hand; the conversation turning to the plan for when they reached landfall. There was little debate before agreement was reached that they hide the ship in Castain's favourite smuggler's cove before scaling the Farthing cliffs, then things got interesting. Aiden was politely making his point about the daftness of showing his face in Astrom and smartly observed, "I'm not saying we can't use my contact, I'm just saying, it wouldn't be smart right now, to show our face's in Astrom."

He was interrupted by a rude reaction from Marlo, the large man laughing in such a manner was random enough, but Marlo gave it special joviality. All in the room waited for Marlo to compose himself, when he finally did his words were laced with mirth, "Don't you see, this is perfect, you can't show your face in Astrom, but we need to go ashore to meet your contact, and it just so happens that the festival of Ardour is starting soon."

It could not be helped that he responded in the tone of a spoilt child, "I may be pretty good at what I do, but I haven't had to dress like a woman yet, and I don't plan to."

Morgan looked like she was about to rebuke him in her typically astute way, but she was beaten to it by Castain who announced gruffly, "As Master at Arms, I am in charge of landing parties, so If I have to wear a dress, you are damn well going to wear one too." He opened his mouth to disagree, but he had seen the look that Castain wore, there was no getting out of this. Closing his mouth, he settled for stamping his foot ever so slightly and petulantly sat back on his chair.

Not skipping a beat, Morgan chose that moment to clarify the plan ensuring all were onboard, in her usual pragmatic manner, "Ok it's settled then. We are going to land at sea, moor the ship in the smuggler's cove, the landing party will then scale the cliff and enter Astrom dressed as women under the guise of attending the festival of Ardour. Anything else to add?" Impressed that Morgan had said her sentence with a straight face, he joined in with talk which quickly turned from business to social, of which happened to be his speciality.

Brady, who surprised him by creeping up from behind, was quickly forgiven when she had the good graces to politely ask him the story of what happened the last time, he was in Astrom. Of course, he obliged diligently. Setting the scene, he started the story early in the piece and finished when he woke on the Serpent, it was then that she exclaimed in surprise, "Are you telling me, Castain not only saved your life once but twice in the space of a month and he even hoisted your horse aboard for you?"

He was one to give credit, where it was due, and so he replied, "I did save his life with my intel more than a few times." The blank look on Brady's face, made him wonder if there was anyone at home upstairs, so he elaborated, "Although sometimes Castain treated me like his badly behaved son, most of the time we were a close-knit team, and we had each other's backs." The room went quiet, pointed stares quickly made him aware that it was his words which had created the hush. Mentally slapping himself, he swallowed and looked towards Morgan. Much to her credit Morgan politely excused herself under the excuse of work. She left with a passive face, as if that was her intent in the first place.

Leaning towards Marlo, he asked, "I didn't mean to offend, should I apologise?"

Marlo wisely replied, "That's ok son, we can all see you have come a long way, I'm sure Morgan didn't take offence, it takes far more than that to offend her." Sighing, he nodded, sitting back in his chair, he made a concerted effort to keep himself out of trouble. Therefore, the rest of the better part of an hour was spent trying to not stare at Meena, an action that he found increasingly hard these days. He usually prided himself in his charms and quite frankly, was skilled at using his charming manner. He was finding himself stuck between worry about what to say to her, and always wanting to be near her. Meena made him a fool by her very presence.

Feeling like he was taking part in a special kind of torture he swallowed, engaged a practised manner and leaned towards her, "I am feeling a lot better now, and I was wondering if we could spar sometime. I think you could help me, defending with the flat edge of my blade could do with some work," he asked politely.

The smile that he produced was usually enough to melt disdain; instead, her reply was typically infuriating yet curious, "You are a horse's arse!"

As he watched Meena walk out in a huff, he could have sworn for a moment her face displayed something other than contempt. Turning towards Marlo he said half in jest, "I thought I was quite handsome, when I look in the mirror, I see myself and go wow!"

Marlo response was to chuckle for a second, and yet as he made an excuse to leave, a secondary reaction of shaking his head continued until he also departed. Left with only a bad feeling and Castain for company, he asked, "What do I do here?"

Castain imparted a heartening response, "Just remember they haven't been stuck with you for as long as I have, so they don't know your humour, just lay off on the charm and stop coming on so strong, aye."

"Me laying on the charm?" he said bewildered.

Castain gave him a stern look and replied, "Yes, you are trying way too hard. It's like you care what these people think." Leaning back in his chair Castain placed two fingers on his chin in a thoughtful manner. After a moment with more surprise than Aiden would have liked, he blurted, "You do, don't you." Hurt by the inference that he was shallow, he sullenly sulked in silence. Castain's next comment sobered him up, somewhat, "Just give it time Aiden, it's still fresh to them, the fact you tried to kill Morgan may still be in their minds." Obligingly he nodded, finding a need for serenity from his unpleasant thoughts, he went to practise with his swords. Although their previous owner had been Meena's father, who was a perfect example of a horse's arse, they had become his favourite possession. Oh yes, it was time to work away more than one kind of frustration.

HAPPY AS ONE could be in her situation; her contentment was borne out of the fact that a well-oiled ship and well-drilled crew were heading toward Sha's rescue. Morgan did not have to look hard to find Meena. She had made a corner of the lower hold her private sanctuary. Walking past a cannon which stood to attention beside a gun port that allowed an expansive view in a volley, Morgan used the aforementioned cannon as a leaning post to take in the impressive sight before her. It was always lovely to watch Meena when she danced with the ribbons. Swords swinging in deadly arc's around the room, she took the opportunity to interrupt Meena, catching her hilts in mid-air. Morgan launched an mki8 opening, "Ok, this can't continue. We need to talk about this. You have been acting out of sorts since we departed and I got to say, this is extreme compared to your normal version of cabin fever."

"No," Meena replied briskly. Lazy sword swings and a tortured look told Morgan that Meena meant something very different.

Watching her friend withdraw from everyone and every-thing in levels far above normal, made her desperate, and so she did something she never did. Taking her tricorne from her head she placed it before her and said, "You know, I never do this but right now I'm not your captain I'm your friend, Meena talk to me."

After an exaggerated sigh to Meena's credit, she did try to voice her thoughts, "I'm feeling so angry, and guilty, and sad. This is all, so damn annoying."

Shocked that Meena had used words describing actual emotion's, a panicked response tumbled from her mouth, luckily she had been practising for the very day Meena admitted she had vulnerability, "Oh Meena that's where you are wrong. Emotions make us more complete-."

Meena cut her off before she could continue with her well-practised speech, "Yes, but you don't understand, it seems to be happening around someone."

The word "someone" was drawn out and caused momentary confusion. Gathering thoughts, Morgan assessed everything Meena had already said. At the point that realisation dawned, there was no stopping her reaction, "With all due respect what is going on, it's like you have a thing for Aiden." She exclaimed in disbelief.

Understanding came too late. Morgan had spoken with little care for her friend's feelings, "Don't use the I'm a relationship expert voice on me. You have only had one relationship, what do you know about it anyway." Meena hissed vehemently.

Holding up her hands in surrender, she said gently, "Woah, oh Meena. You do have feels for him. I'm so sorry, please just give me a sec to process." Using the cannon to prop herself up, she gripped her hat as if it was a lifeline to sanity. Up until now, she could count on Meena's relationships to be short and measured in days, depending on what he did wrong but this was different, she could see fear and doubt on her friend's face. Feelings of protectiveness and even momentary jealously was swept aside. Looking up she took in her very much deflated friend, "I can see what this is doing to you, and you have a tendency to be negative about your relationships so I'm going to ask, what is the problem here Meena?" She asked gently.

In reply and on cue, Meena started to list all of Aiden's flaws, "I'm pissed at him for leaving with Castain without a backwards glance. I thought we had a moment and then just like that, he was just gone, he's a snob, is handsome and knows it. Plus he's way too self-assured."

Waiting until Meena took a breath, she interrupted, "Ok I'm going to stop you right there because we could be here for a while. It's clear this situation is different, so let me give you some advice I have been wanting to give you, for ages," Walking up to stand squarely in front, she placed her hands on Meena's shoulders. She said, "If you are always saying what you don't want, you are not opening up yourself, to everything you do want."

The screwing up of Meena's face made it evident that she neither understood, nor cared for her extremely apt advice. Sighing, she continued, "look, I know you well enough to know this is all false bravado. I can't make you believe that you deserve to be happy. Do me a favour and next time you walk past a mirror don't avoid it take a good look, I know what you think you see, let me tell you what everyone else sees, a beautiful, dedicated, loyal, fierce woman who deserves happiness." Feeling pleased with herself she left a bewildered-looking Meena, and strode towards her office, her contentment was short-lived however, when it dawned on her that her momentary excuse to hide from warring thoughts was over.

COLOUR AND COURAGE

*N*earing the end of a long dry summer, it was about as good of a day, as one could be in the current climate. Ranger was on his back, sunning himself in his favourite post chore spot. Minus a shirt, he was hidden by the long grass of the farms front paddock. Eyes closed, he casually chewed on the end of a piece of grass, suffice to say he was more than happy to be lost in thoughts that took him away from the type of worries that a nineteen-year-old, should not have. He was more than old enough to be wed, although if his mum wasn't so picky, he would be. Like any boy his age, his thoughts were on his current crush. Jayna was a pretty girl from Jerone. Whenever he visited the village, she would often look up from the washing trough and gift him a smile. Of course, he envisioned Jayna's smiles were saved only for him. Rightly so, he worked hard and being that he was of age and an only child, he was a valuable prospect for any village girl. Smelling the dry fresh scent of the grass around him, the impending end to his rest caused a sigh to escape, long and drawn out he almost didn't hear the sound of approaching riders. Although they were in no hurry, the farm was out of the way for most, so he curiously popped his head above the grass. It quickly became evident, however, that he should have stayed hidden. Riding up the long dirt track that led to the farmyard was six hooded figures, he had never seen them before, but he had heard enough stories to know the vacant-eyed hooded robe types, never showed up for a friendly visit. Before he knew it, the stalk had come flying out of his mouth, and his legs were taking him towards the farmhouse. As the grass whipped past him, his thoughts turned to the reason for their visit, none of the options was acceptable. Among the most likely were that they required slaves, needed conscripts or they had heard you showed promise as a caster of darkness. Rumour had it if you were unlucky enough to be picked for training, they took you to Hero's fall. Hero's fall was a foreboding tower inconveniently located in the middle of the Leviraan dessert. After your training, if your family saw you again, it was as a lifeless shell. He had a pretty good idea of why they had decided to visit his quiet corner of Sirillia. Before being taken away, he desperately needed to say goodbye to his parents. Without meaning too and quite distressingly at times, unusual things happened around him.

Up until recently, the randomness happened when he was in the confines of the farm; therefore, only his parents knew his secret. That was until, at the last village gathering, an unintended side effect of a stolen kiss with Jayna, caused every fire and torch to unnaturally flare, so intense was the brightness that a moonless night turned into day. Unfavourable Rumours quickly spread in his direction, and clearly, the story had made its way to the evil that was about to reach his doorstep. As his feet hit their smooth surface, the cobles of the farmyard caused a momentary loss of traction. He was so rushed that his long legs sent him inside boots and all. His mother looked up from the bed she was making in surprise, a sternness on her face at the sight of his dirty boots was not followed by reprimand. His expression must have disclosed the terror sadness and even anger that he felt. Heartened by the sight of his father sorting through tack across the room, he slammed the door and pulled the bolt across. Joining in on his Mother's worried glance, his father straightened and said in alarm, "What is it, son?"

He opened his mouth to answer, but instead, an abrupt demand came from the other side of the bolted door, "Open up and relinquish the magic-user." Pale-faced his Mother raced over and attached herself protectively to him, she was small however, so she only managed to claim one side. Stuck as to what to say or do, he absently placed his arm around his mother. His father strode towards the opposite side of the room. Taking up arms his father posted himself between door and son, the resigned look upon his face confirmed that this was an eventuality he had been expecting. Panicked feelings raced through his brain, his simple happy life was falling apart and he could do nothing but stand there dumbstruck, gone was the feeling that this was happening elsewhere, it was now literally on his doorstep.

The only action before him despite wanting to run and cry or do something even more idiotic was to take a step towards the door. His Mother to clung tighter, "No, they can't have you," She cried.

Not bothering to turn, his father brandished his pitchfork menacingly and said, "Stand behind me, son."

Sounding more bored than impatient, the lead aggressor said from outside, "Come out, or we will set the house on fire and you will all die, either way, we get some sport."

The threatening statement left him with the sad realization that there was only one way to save his parents and that was to lose himself, he just needed to talk them into letting him go before they all died. As he opened his mouth to try and articulate his feelings, he was cut off again, this time for a different reason, a small child had materialized into existence between his father and the bolted door. Roughly dressed in tattered cotton, the child smelt like she had come in from herding sheep. All knew without explanation who their visitor was and what her presence meant. The look on the small child's face was too serious for one so young, yet she exuded calm and her voice cut through the worry that owned the room, "Do not fear parents of Ranger, this is his destiny."

For a moment no one moved, then thankfully his father looked towards the child and relaxed, rotating his fork around until upright, he woodenly moved away from the doorway. His father's nod towards the girl was respectful, yet sadness marred his worn features. Not ready to let go, when he felt his Mother's arms loosen he responded by squeezing her, as if the hug were his last. Reaching out with his other arm his father rewarded him with a rare embrace. Holding onto the feeling as long as he dared, he released. Nearly paralyzed by what he had to do, he found the strength to take a step towards the door. Feeling bile in his throat the step was enough for fear to get the better of him and he halted. A small warm hand grabbed a few of his much larger fingers, as he looked down at the face of the child her uplifting but cryptic words warmed him, "Don't worry Ranger, I am always with you, just do me a favour will you, look up after the declaration of love." Absently nodding, he found the strength to take the final step then placing his hands on the bolt he pulled it across. Looking low, the small child and her comforting presence was gone. To the background noise of his now blubbering Mother, he walked outside, time to meet the darkness and his destiny before him.

.   .   .

BLENDING in was as easy as joining the steady trail of men and woman making the journey from the surrounding desert. Castain personally felt the idea of a gathering to find a mate to assuage loneliness was a little archaic. He understood the necessity most of the tribesman lived in tight-knit roving groups; unless you wanted to marry an undesired cousin, you needed to undertake such pilgrimages. From what he understood the festival of Ardour wasn't just about finding a partner, it was also to worship Anene, the goddess of beginnings and relationships. The desert tribes also believed that Anene would one day make an appearance to renew their lands and bring redemption. He understood that Anene was one of their most adored deity's, what he found odd however was that she was said to be a gentle, childlike goddess who enjoyed the company of baby animals. The atmosphere and kaleidoscope of colour in the distance, caused a memory burst into his mind. It was one he was happy to contemplate, a memory from a period just after his nineteenth birthday when things were carefree and straightforward; he would often hide with the woman he loved from responsibilities and eyes. Overlooking the throne room was a balcony very few knew of, where they would sit, talk, and look towards candelabras and pennants in the many colours of the kingdom below. Because his father had insisted upon it, his life had consisted of training to be a King's Guardsman, and more importantly ever-increasing yet stolen moments with his love. Mira would often look at him in a carefree way that inferred she also felt their problems were a world away. By that stage and despite his youth, he had already made a name for himself as the best fighter in the kingdom and because of such, had quickly gained favour with the king who had appointed him as his personal squire. Such an elevation in a lowly noble caused jealously among the up-and-coming Guard, one of which was his royal highness Fife Jorn Dallinger. Often Mira would cheer him up after a typical attempt by Fife to undermine his good esteem with a heartening and sometimes scandalous comment, usually she accompanied her remarks by rolling her eyes or smiling mischievously. Despite her fine northern upbringing Mira treated other nobles with disdain. On such occasions, he would put an arm around her and say, "Why don't we just leave this behind, my plotted life as a Kings Guard and yours as the wife of some higher than thou gentry?"

Her answer was always the same, "Because you would not be happy and neither would I, despite how hard you try to hide it you live for a life of servitude to the crown, and I would lose the trust of my parents, whom I dearly love."

Shunted out of his reverie, Aiden spoke in a scandalized tone, "Hello Castain, didn't you hear me, how is one supposed to find a husband in this get up? I look like a rainbow vomited, and the mask, you can only see my eye's, what's the point."

He replied with a straight face, despite an inner child wanting to do the opposite, "It's all about leaving something to the imagination. Besides what are you worried about, your eyes are your best asset. You are highly likely to snap up a rich husband with your combination of looks and prospects."

Shocked Aiden blinked in his direction, then retorted sarcastically, "Did you just crack a joke, whoa, that's your one for the year, what are you going to do for the rest of the year, brood grumpily with more gusto than normal." He raised an eyebrow, then realized no one could see it. Unfortunately, Aiden took his silence as an opening and continued, "If I had my way this dress would be way more fitting you would be able to see my curves or stunning legs at the least, it all seems a little unfair on the poor unsuspecting man."

Quickly losing patience, he replied, "This isn't about

advertising ourselves Aiden, we are dressed this way as a disguise."

Not taking the subtle hint of the harshness in his voice, Aiden continued, "But I'm just saying."

Finally snapping he cut Aiden off, all the while feeling like he was showing his age, "Aiden, have you ever heard of the saying, why have the milk when you can have the cow for free, you might as well give away the whole herd." Thankful for Aiden's sudden silence, he continued to focus on his disguise, never had he thought that he would have to put so much energy into not walking like a man. Memory now faded, he left it where it rightly belonged, with all the other could have been future possibilities.

DEFIANCE

$\mathcal{B}$rutally reminded that teaching was his least favourite task, Marlo had spent the better part of the afternoon, training Tanner to operate the ship. Despite Tanner's brilliance, his constant questions were at times infuriating, now was no different. He was amidst an explanation on the finer points of lift and thrust when he saw that Morgan's party was back from their fact-finding mission. Grateful for the break, he excused himself and left Tanner to prep for voyage and eventual lift away. Although outwardly Morgan did not show it, he knew her well enough to know something was amiss, "Where to Captain?" He asked carefully, drawing her out.

"We head for Leviraan desert with all haste. The enemy came through here, nearly a month ago," Morgan replied.

Morgan's disheartening reply caused him to forget himself and he blurted panicked words, "No, no, no that has to be a mistake. Everyone knows you don't go there, its death, not to mention there is a big tower in the centre that is surrounded in death."

"Yes, I know, that is our heading," Morgan replied distantly.

Tanner had already piloted the ship out of the cove, and Morgan's voice sounded sombre in the waiting darkness, "Harness and lift away." The shrill call of the bosun's whistle warned of impending ascent. On queue the deck transformed into a flurry of activity, all went about duties or obediently escaped below decks. Feeling silly, he closed his mouth. Morgan's bearing as she walked away told him all he needed to know; the oppression before her was a heavy burden.

AFTER A DRAWN-OUT and gruelling few day's Morgan was happy to learn that the edge of the Leviraan desert was in sight, in less than a week she would have answers, retribution and hopefully Sha's presence. The mind focusing task of pounding her practise dummy was sending sweat dripping into her eyes. It was amidst a flurry of punches that Taymah raced in. Impatiently rocking on the balls of her feet, Taymah waited for the completion of a jab before declaring, "Captain, you are needed urgently at the port rail."

Hurriedly she grabbed a towel and raced to the indicated rail, there she met up with Castain who was harnessed and staring intensely over the side. The object of his stare caused her to yell loudly in alarm. "Gruth descend now, get as close as possible!"

Before she could bark further orders, Castain surprised her by stating, "Your landing party is ready Captain." Nodding, she tapped her foot impatiently and surveyed the sight below, absorbed in a search for signs of life.

Beneath the ship, a circle of upright pillars stuck out in stark contrast to the moving desert around them, chained to every pillar high above the ground was a score of exposed souls, each stripped bare and left to the extreme temperatures the desert provided. Despite a hasty landing and her crew's speedy ability to check for signs of life, only one man showed signs of life. As the poor soul was carefully lowered to the blessed ground, his muscular arms taunt by the elevated position went slack and he slumped weakly. Waiting for him to be carefully propped up, she brought a flask to his lips and was pleased when he drank. Then as Taymah gently placed a cover over his dry burnt skin, the ailing man pushed outwards with his arms, finding buried strength to fight attempts of aid, opening his eyes, he said croakily, "No you have to leave me, I have to die."

Assuming the poor man's ramblings were side effects of delirium and not wanting to linger, Morgan called for him to be hoisted aboard. Once there, he leaned against the starboard rail and stared dumbly at the oppressive wooden graveyard that he had been liberated from moments earlier. She called for lift away as she walked past her inquisitive crew, they scurried to life leaving her with the ship's new visitor. Unsure of the man's mental state, she curiously watched for clues, darting eyes and a dazed demeanour told her that he was frightened. Not sensing anything untoward, she sat down beside him and secured him to the closest anchor point. A short visual assessment told her much, this young sandy-haired man was used to a day's work, he was tall and had well-formed muscles, yet the way he held himself inferred he had not fought a day in his life, aside from burnt skin and dehydration he was in surprisingly good shape. Keeping her voice even, she said gently, "it's even better at night, almost as if you are keeping the moon company." Her comment drew a bewildered expression, happy he was not addled she continued, "What is your name friend, and why were you chained up in such a fashion?"

The man replied, "My name is Ranger, that." Ranger

pointed towards the pillars, "Is what they do to anyone who has been particularly bad and goes against the master's rules."

"What rule did you break Ranger?" She asked, unsure if she wanted to know the answer.

"I refused to train in magic at Hero's end, the tower in the middle of the desert," Ranger replied, sounding distant.

A chill ran down her spine, mostly because his comment reminded her of a statement she had been conveniently ignoring in Bella's letter. Deciding it was a good idea to give Ranger some space from her inquisitive crew, she asked for Cheese to take him to a spare officer's cabin and ensure he had everything he needed. Her hastened stride quickly took her to her cabin, where she paced until it felt silly. She grabbed her staff in an effort to exercise her thoughts into quiet; it was then that she noticed a pronounced hum in the back of her mind. Instinct told her that the staff was responding to her fear. Yes, she was just going to have to admit that she was well and truly out of her element.

She watched Ranger protectively, despite her command to the opposite, he was quickly singled out by the Tempest's more brazen crew members. Before a day had passed the ship was awash with rumours, most of which centred around the real reason for his survival. Ranger was among the elements for over three days. Most of her crew's complaints stemmed from the fact that they did not believe Ranger's story and therefore thought him crazy or a liar, she did not blame them, up until Bella's letter she would have shared their opinion. Despite evident shyness Ranger bore well under the pressure, sarcastically toned jokes about the fact that his name was not befitting of an acolyte, were taken in his stride and as soon as he got over the shock of being on a flying ship he flourished. Ranger was clearly no stranger to hard work, quickly busying his blistered hands to manual labour, despite his weakness and lack of knowledge, he made up for any shortcomings with effort and eagerness. Her observations left her with the impression that Ranger was a man driven to find anything to occupy his time, to the point that he often ignored his own needs. Morgan knew without asking, Ranger's busyness was more than just fastidiousness, it was a concerted effort to think about anything other than their destination. Amidst it all, her staff was constant in its hum; she knew it was because the fear of the unknown had bloomed and become known in her heart.

HARD AT WORK merely minding his own business Aiden was training in the Lower hold, an expected task on the ship which he was happy to engage in. Meena was finally allowing him to train in the same area as her, as long of course, that he did not encroach. The fact that Meena was ignoring him with less viciousness every day was heartening. Meena had even stopped long enough to comment on his footwork during a jab, he had been too shocked to thank her, yet he was thankful nonetheless. Happy at his work, it was just as the sweat was starting to drip down his bare torso that he heard the tell-tale giggle coming from behind him. Clenching his teeth, he sighed and turned to see the expected sight of his groupies admiring him. Feeling like a piece of meat Aiden was about to turn back to his work when Meena came storming past and up the stairs, shattered he could say nothing but sheathe his sword and walk away from the gawping. Sidling over to Tanner who was checking a cannon, he said frustratingly, "Do you understand woman, because I have recently come to the conclusion, that I have absolutely no idea!"

Tanner smiled and replied, "You're damn right about that my friend, take your groupies for example, Brady likes girls and is using you to follow Taymah around, who she has a crush on."

Shocked, he replied, "How does that work?"

It was as he realised how silly his comment sounded, that Tanner replied indignant, "Well if you don't know, I'm certainly not going to tell you."

"No, that's not what I meant." He stammered, Tanner however, was already exiting in a hurry to get to his next job, panic arose amidst the sudden realisation, that he had been left alone with his groupies. It was as he was contemplating his escape, that Ameile walked down the stairs to join in on the infuriating giggling. Eyes levelled hungrily on his sweaty chest, Like Aquila narrowing in on his prey the gaggle started to walk towards him. "Ah sorry ladies, got to go, I've got to take a bath, I'm so, so dirty," He exclaimed. Noting how high his voice sounded, Aiden left, hurried along by the fact the sight of his behind was enough to set them off again in a chorus of eww's and ahh's. Wondering what he had ever done to deserve such scandalous behaviour, he raced up the stairs taking them two, then three at a time. After reaching the deck he harnessed himself and took a long slow deliberate breath. It was as he was starting to regain composure, that the thud, of a newly deceased hare hit the deck, squealing in surprise, he looked up. Aquila's squawk greeted him.

Waiting long enough for the bird to land on the rail beside him, he scolded, "Why can't you just tenderise your food on land, like most birds."

The bird's frustrating reply was along the lines of, that is the thanks I get for bringing a message all this way.

"Well, it's about time you showed up," He re-joined.

The bird's snippy reply was unrepeatable.

"Well, there's no need to be so rude," He rebuked, taking

the letter, he waited for Aquila to fly up to his usual perch, before he went in search of Morgan, for delivery.

THE ARRIVAL of Aquila and his letter elevated Morgan's terse nerves, lifting the parchment she grabbed her reading glass to read her friend's tiny words.

DEAR FRIEND, whom I sorely miss,

BY NOW YOU have made landfall upon Sirillia, I am sure it's nothing, but something Leo said to me caused me to scour all the texts you have had me search for any information on the weapons which we wield, oh, by the way, I also have one now. The only thing I could find was a vague paragraph written by an eccentric monk about weapons of legend. They were blessed by the gods and made by the children of light, whoever they are. What gave me pause, was that the paragraph went on to state that such weapons only surface at a time of great need. Sounds very worrying but I would greatly appreciate if you could always keep yours on you, as well as Meena and Aiden.

YOUR FRIEND BELLA

PS – When you find Sha, please tell him Leo is ok and misses him.

AFTER PUTTING THE LETTER DOWN, Morgan felt a pang of loss for her absent friend. Bella's growing love for Leo was apparent in her carefree writing style. Brushing off a fleeting smile she got down to business. Snatching her staff, she affixed the sheath Marlo had made for her and went on a search for Meena and Aiden who would be on opposite sides of the ship. It was time to make an entirely unfounded but ominous request, that they must always keep their weapons close.

AFTER THEY REACHED what he assumed was their destination, there had been a distinct change in his captor's behaviour. The cold dark grey tower that dominated the desert-scape caused hope to fade; it didn't help that immediately after arrival he was marched into a cell and left with only darkness and his noises to keep him company. Sha's first impression was that his captors were a bunch of boring idiots. A clear example of lazy styling, bare sandstone walls, floors, and ceilings greeted him. It was what he assumed was a day later, as he contemplated licking water off the wall that he heard an unfamiliar sound echoing around him. Straining to hear, it took moments to realise the sound was in fact footfalls coming in his direction, settling himself against the wall in a defiantly casual position he waited for his visitor. When the echo's turned into shapes, one shape stood out from the others. The ominous sight of waves of darkness were scaring away any torchlight that attempted to illuminate a figure that stood before him. "Well met princeling, I am Aidis king of the Dark Acolytes, impressive that you can pretend you are not bothered by your situation, even when it is hopeless." The untoward visitor announced. His words disheartening to say the least, were made worse by the way they made Sha's skin crawl.

"I wouldn't bother if I were you, I think perhaps you should just go ahead and kill me because you are mistaken if you think you can turn me," he said defiantly, attempting a bravado that he did not feel.

Although he could not see it, he knew the hooded figure smiled by the tone of his reply, "This staff, can do the very thing you are saying, I am unable to do."

It was then that Sha noticed the unnaturally shiny, black, short staff which the figure held. Typically, he replied using his default setting of humour, "Look, what you do with your short stubby staff in your spare time is entirely up to you, I'm not really into that sort of thing, I would prefer if you left me out of it."

Aidis's growl brought happiness, yet it was short-lived as what Aidis said next sent a chill down his spine, "You have already served your purpose. I don't need you for anything from this point other than to serve as amusement, and I can say assure you, your pain will be very amusing to me." With only a moment to let the words sink in, he was roughly grabbed by the two burly types Aidis had brought with him, then in an entirely unfair manner he was held in place as Aidis approached. He fought and momentarily broke contact, that was until the staff reached the vicinity of his skin. It started as a searing burn, then at a simple touch elevated to unimaginable pain. His legs buckled under the strain of a fire that burnt every fibre of his being, still it continued. Curled up into a hopeless ball, it continued still, until finally consciousness was lost. Unfortunately, that was not the end of his suffering the dreams that followed, gave him haunting memories of an overwhelming pain, that would not stop. Sleep was restless and fitful, yet when he felt that he was helplessly lost to pain and tortured memory, he was visited in his dreams by a friend. The friend had Nia's face, yet he knew from the gift of peace and welcome rest, that it was not her.

HOLY SHIP

*P*ersistent in his nagging, Aiden followed him up onto the quarter deck despite the fact he was trying to escape. The puppy dog look upon Aiden's face wasn't working, so he was using his best pleading tone, "Come on Castain, I need your help here, just a little roleplay that's all I'm asking."

"NO!" he snapped, finite in his reply.

Annoyingly the pestering continued, "Please, Please, Please Castain think of it as payback for when I saved your life at that tavern in Gradia."

The incident in question was irrelevant because he had saved Aiden's life many more times over, if there were in fact, a tally, he would be winning hands down. He was however, aware of the repercussions of pretending there was an end to Aiden's annoying requests, and so he relinquished, "Ok, but you owe me, next time, you will leave me to my break in peace or I will hang you to the kite sail by your underpants."

"Alright, you be Meena, and I will be me," Aiden said, without skipping a beat or applying gratitude.

"Just get on with it," He growled.

Ignoring his obvious tone, Aiden pushed his shoulders back and spoke as if practising with an unwilling friend was something he did every day, and not something he was doing because he was deathly scared of speaking to a woman.

"Hi, Meena," Aiden said, starting strong.

"Hi, horses arse," Castain replied, getting himself into character.

Aiden stopped momentarily, then shrugged as if in acceptance that Meena would speak in such a manner, then he politely asked, "How are you today?"

"Stop wasting my time. What do you want?" He replied, starting to enjoy himself.

"I was wondering if we could get to know each other better" Aiden said, with all sincerity.

"Oh sure, Aiden. I sure would love that." He replied. Placing his palms together, he feigned excitement while fighting to keep the smile off his face.

"No, No, No, that's not what she would say at all, you need to be more aggressive," Aiden said, berating him for his efforts.

Deciding it was high time to give Aiden, what he was so desperately asking for, he replied in kind, "Do I look like the talking type, shit for brains." Punching Aiden solidly in the shoulder for effect, he waited for the consequence.

Aiden blinked momentarily surprised, then rubbing the sore spot he protested, "Damn it Castain, why would you do that. Forget this. Wish me luck."

As he watched Aiden stomp away, he felt happy the interaction was over and anything but lucky to be a party to it. Casually he leaned on the rail fully intending to get back to post annoyance relaxing. Marlo, who was at the wheel, choose that moment to matter-of-factly state, "He's in deep, deep water, I hope she doesn't have a weapon handy."

Nodding in agreement to Marlo's comment he turned

back in time to catch the interaction between Aiden and Meena. Meena was above board on a rare break from duties and training, on a slow approach, Aiden carefully sidled over, as if afraid of catching her unawares. He did not need to overhear the conversation, to have a fair idea of what was going on. Aiden seemed to give Meena a cordial greeting, she then replied in what he assumed was her standard gruff retort. To his surprise, Aiden didn't beat around the bush and spoke about his request to talk; he knew this because the response was regrettable and precisely as he had anticipated. Meena's sound punch was delivered where it had been moments earlier and was followed by her storming off in a huff. Most on the deck heard Aiden's frustrated rant, "What's with the women on this ship."

Happy that his friend had learnt that the best things in life were worth waiting for, he sat down with his back to the rail. The tortured look on Aiden's face reminded him, of himself at a similar age. Leaning back and closing his eyes, he let himself remember a time when life was perfect right up until it wasn't. He even remembered the exact moment when his life veered sharply from planned and structured to chaotic. He was hauled before the King after an unfortunate incident that had resulted in a bloody nose. Unfortunately, it was him that gifted the bloody nose, the crown prince the recipient. Castain had been the most surprised by his actions, Herne was his friend, and never had he thought he would find himself in a fight, for none other than the right to court Mira. It was a done deal in his mind that he would be exiled on the spot. His liege was wise and fair and had given him a choice, one he was eternally grateful for, he was to either leave the kingdom never to return or redeem himself by undertaking a dangerous mission to investigate rumours of a threat on the continent of Sirillia. It was strongly suggested that he be gone a few years to let things die down, even though his heart had constricted at the thought of releasing Mira to a life without him, he loved his King and felt there was no other choice. Always the dutiful weapon he had left to throw himself into his task, the heart he left behind he never found again. A short time after that, he had received news of Mira and Herne's engagement. What had seemed so easy at the time had shaped his life in every way since.

Usually, he was happy to be brought out of such unhappy memories. Still, the loud noises that emitted from the side of the ship as if close cannon fire was impacting were enough to wake the dead. The ship came alive, the confused calls of the crew mixed with searing heat from a dark bolt of energy soaring past. Chunks of wood flew around him, where the burning darkness impacted it destroyed. The ship shuddered as a bolt hit one of the four main rope lines melting a few of the many supports. Snapping to action Castain leapt down the stairs to inspect the damage quickly assessing that it was already half gone, "MARLO, THE STARBOARD AFT CABLE IS ABOUT TO SNAP, WE HAVE TO TAKE THE STRAIN AWAY NOW." Loud consecutive cracking noises closely followed his alarmed yell, each of the final layers of support snapped beside him. The ship vibrated violently then lurched to one side, hit by something harder and with more force, than he had ever experienced, and immense pain shunted him towards oblivions waiting arms.

MORGAN HAD JUST BEEN UNCEREMONIOUSLY THROWN to the floor, the ship was lurching hard and the furniture in her office seemed to be trying to crush her. Snatching her staff as it rolled towards her, she clutched, grabbed, and pushed herself against anything that was available to get towards the doorway. After reaching the threshold she was struck by a frantic scene, harnessed crew members scrambled to keep the ship aloft most working on adding stability by tying ropes, others desperately shortening harness lines in an effort to secure themselves. A loud roar told her Marlo had sent all power to the aft mast tubes, before she could take another step, the ship impacted with the ground. Flattened against the deck she tasted blood, a result of her chin striking floorboards. In the process of getting back to her feet she was again thrown downwards, the ship continued to skid like a skipping stone upon the desert floor and she was similarly bounced around. Smartly staying down until it was safe to stand, she spat blood out of her mouth, groaning she pushed with her arms and legs. She intended to help any that required aid, Aroon met her as she stepped over the threshold, his panicked eye's caused her to grip her staff tighter in alarm. He spoke fear laced words, "Captain, a group of black-robed figures attacked us from the desert below. They sent dark blasts towards us, and one broke one of the main cables-" Aroon did not complete his report because chaos began to reign.

Loud booms assaulted Morgan's ears as if something were trying to destroy the hull one blast at a time. She knew it was the dark acolytes, taking charge she commanded, "unharness, take cover or get below decks, now!" Her barked command drew a flurry of fire which seemed to be arching around the ship to reach her, as if those sending them could aim them without the need for sighting their target. Grabbing Aroon's shirt, she roughly pulled him inside as blasts continued to pepper the outside cabin causing splinters to fly everywhere. Feeling a fool, she hid using the inside wall for cover, unable to do nought but yell orders through an open doorway, in the vain hope it would draw fire away from those vacating the deck. Flinching as wood splintered from the door jamb, she felt the sting of the resulting cuts upon her face.

Desperately Morgan searched her mind for any plan that might save everyone from one of the many unfortunate eventualities racing through her head. Panic set in, her excessive training, control, and planning eventuated in nothing but racing thoughts. She knew death was very near and she could do nothing to delay it. A sheen of sweat coated her brow, and she froze. Amidst defeat, hopelessness gripped her heart. Her staff's previously distant hum was demanding her attention, firmly vibrating from staff to mind, instinct told her it was attempting to give her answers. She took the only option that remained, focusing her thoughts upon the sound, possibilities she had never imagined replaced crippling fear. The alignment left her with blessed clarity, for once in her life she relied on something other than her own perfectly planned internal directions. Standing up amongst the chaos, she spun her staff before her causing bolts of energy to bounce in all directions, nothing permeated her shield, nor was she surprised by its appearance. With renewed purpose, she stepped forward and leapt over the rail, landing on the desert floor, as if the considerable height was nothing.

The eye of the storm Morgan calmly and intuitively reigned lethal carnage upon her foes, feeling more than seeing Aiden and Meena at her back her enemies continued to fall in a rightly unfair manner, then just like that it was over. Perusing the scene invited guilt, it was never her intention to kill, however the weapons seemed to have chosen a few targets to melt before her eyes leaving an inky dark substance, others were left knocked out and unharmed. Sighing a wave of weariness washed over her, unconsciously smearing blood across her cheek with her hand, she went in search of a status report.

It was Marlo who found her first, he blurted incredulous, "what just happened, I mean, you just used your staff to send a guy's bolt of energy back at him, you melted his face, melted his face, Morgan!" Marlo took a breath, his panic had not subsided as when he continued he nearly forgot to breathe, "And Meena, Meena, she did that spinning thing with her ribbons, which sent her swords in deadly arc's all over the place, she took out so many at once, so, so, many. Not to mention that thing Aiden did, I mean he threw his sword, and it came back like a dog, like a dog Morgan!"

By this stage, Marlo was hysterical, so she patted his arm reassuringly while he sucked in air and calmly said, "Marlo, I don't have time for your hysterics."

Feeling him relax, she was about to speak, when reading her mind, Marlo stammered, "You want me to fix the ship, don't you?"

Grateful, she replied, "Yes, Marlo, that would be nice, report back when you know how long we are going to be stuck here."

Moving to oblige, he wagged his finger in disapproval, grumbling under his breath, "We are going to talk about this later." Nodding, she watched him leave, grateful for his intuitiveness and care.

It was Brady who found her next. The concern in Brady's voice caused her to listen with elevated intensity as her report went on, "Captain, we have two dead and another six that are more serious otherwise the superficial injuries have been brought onto the deck." Brady's hesitation made her heart flutter, then Brady continued, "Castain is one of the six, he has the worst injuries we took him to his cabin. Captain, it is bad."

Ignoring the feeling that were threatening to overwhelm, she issued Brady's orders, "Get Gruth, to see to, the rest of the more serious Injuries, I will see to Castain, you can handle the superficial."

Waiting long enough for Brady's affirmation, she engaged tired legs in an effort to get to Castain and Aiden's shared cabin. Those who tried to converse with her were background noise, discarded by a singular focus. She was surprised by the fear Castain's possible death brought, yet deep down she knew the uncomfortable truth.

Morgan walked into the cabin where she found Aiden staring at his lifeless friend who was resting on blood-stained sheets. Aiden had applied a tourniquet to Castain's crushed leg but seemed unsure of what to do next, "The anchor point, it blew off the side of the ship and crushed his leg," He mumbled when he registered her presence.

Knowing her best option was to focus Aiden's mind, she gave him instruction, "Go and get the medical box from my day room." When he hesitated, she stated, "don't worry Aiden, I've got this."

As she busied her eyes in an assessment of the damage, worry deepened, Castain's left leg split in a gruesome and spectacular fashion, worse still he had lost a lot of blood. When Aiden returned, she sent him for hot water, cold water, fresh blankets on it continued, all to keep him out of her way. The hours passed by, and she meticulously cleaned, reset and stitched. Aiden had long since fallen asleep in the corner by the time her work was complete. Bandaging a leg held together by cuts, bruises and stitches, she carefully refreshed the bed around him. Her hands shook from fatigue as she took another look at her father's face, not fooled by calm features, his pallor and sustained unconscious state, left her feeling unworthy. Desperately wishing her search for Nia had been fruitful, realisation dawned that despite all her toil if Castain were to die, then it would be soon. She was determined to sit in vigil and before long she found herself holding Castain's hand. Her body betrayed her, exhaustion took over, and she fell into a fatigue-induced slumber.

BLACK ROSE

It was early morning when Morgan woke. Her first alarming thought was on the fact that even her morning coffee wouldn't scare away the furriness in her mouth, it was as she was executing a pleasing stretch, that she realised she was still at Castain's bedside. Panic set in and Morgan held her breath hoping to see the very thing that moments later occurred, Castain took a distinct breath, the simple act caused hope to rise and her own chest followed suit. Then she saw the tell-tale sweaty sheen upon his brow, swearing she looked around for a cold compress, as if reading her mind Aiden appeared with the very thing. After sitting beside, Aiden dipped the cloth, squeezed and gently dabbed, meeting her eye he gave her the slightest of nods and said with gratitude laced words, "I've got this Morgan, go and stretch your legs, Aroon has been waiting for you to wake, he is in the upper hold along with the rest of the officers."

Although it was more challenging than she cared to admit, she nodded and went about her duties. As always Meena came through, the coffee appeared before her as she stepped into the hallway, smiling gratefully in return,

Meena's only response was to fall in, clearly aware of her destination. As she walked into the hold, a strange sight greeted her, Ranger was on his hands and knees, before an unconscious and unhooded black cloak, "Wow, she is still stunning." Meena said in awe, only adding to the surreal nature of the situation.

It was Marlo who said what everyone was thinking, "Meena, do you ever look into a mirror?" Marlo waited for Meena's typical shrug, accompanied by a pfft noise, before continuing, "Captain, this is Lashima, Princess of the Reshda tribe. She is the very same contact that was supposed to meet us before we got attacked by black cloaks in Astrom. I think it is obvious what held her up that day. She was knocked unconscious in the battle yesterday."

Perusing the woman who had drawn everyone's attention, large eyes, high cheekbones and suntanned skin added together to equal a rare desert flower. Lashima's peaceful expression caused a pang of regret for those who had not been lucky enough to be taken prisoner, even in her restrained state a regal bearing was evident. The only detractor from the woman's beauty was the black dots which ran vertically from forehead to cheek, curious she asked, "Ranger, tell me why you are bowing to this woman, her tribe isn't close to yours?"

"She is the desert rose," Ranger replied matter-of-factly, not bothering to lift his head to speak.

She was about to request an explanation, but the woman awoke, and despite being bound, deftly leapt to her feet and charged towards Morgan with a focus she would have envied If it wasn't for the fact she was hell-bent on killing her. Embarrassingly and because of her lack of warning, her instinct was to bring up her staff in defence, the result was as confusing as it was surprising, as Lashima contacted the staff she crumpled to the ground. Staring dumbly between staff and regal heap, she was surprised to see the Princess had even managed to collapse in a dignified way. Curious she stepped forward and pressed her staff against the mound upon the ground, the surreal result was writhing and jerking for a few moments, then sudden limpness. Amidst the considerably quieter room, the Princess opened her eyes and spoke grateful words, "Thank you, Morgan, I thought I would be stuck like that forever, I was so close to losing myself."

Lashima's comment brought with it the realisation that her staff had done whatever Nia's potion did in a very effective manner. Taking the dots disappearing from Lashima's face as confirmation, she requested the Princess be unbound and made comfortable, then in awareness of Ranger who was still bowing she politely asked, "Princess this is Ranger. Please put him out of his misery I think he's getting sore knees."

Lashima seemed to see him for the first time; guilt momentarily graced her face, then she smiled, the effect made her more beautiful, if she had powers hers would be stopping time with gorgeousness. "Hello Ranger, I can only assume by the bowing that you know my other title, please rise friend." Lashima said kindly, meeting the gazes of many in the room, "I would appreciate, if you could all just call me Lash," She asked, reaching her hand out to help Ranger up.

The expression Ranger wore upon his face said everything, hesitantly he took the offered hand and rose, stepping backwards he awkwardly tried to hide amongst the onlookers. Morgan waited for Lash to meet her eye then asked pointedly, "It seems you know me, but I am at a loss here, we have never actually met."

Lash's genuine smile and relaxed demeanour showed she was used to being the centre of attention. Accepting water Lash made herself comfortable by leaning against the nearest barrel then she spoke to the room of onlookers as if they were already friends, "I know you because I did my home-work before requesting to meet you. I was captured right after meeting Marlo and Meena at the Bazaar, soon after Kurja died, the black cloaks were sent to serve another master. I was still fighting for my mind at that stage, and like a pre-planned operation, they were pulled towards Hero's End. That's where I lost the battle." Lash used no embellish-ment, nor did she need to. Morgan felt a growing respect for the woman before her, "My journey from that point was like thousands before me. Every kill for the Master took me further away from redemption and my people's salvation. I had heard the whispers and stories to frighten children of course, but like most, I was unaware of what lay in wait at Hero's end. The King of what I heard you call the Dark Acolytes knows no equal in his arrogance, and if you thought Kurja was bad, Aidis is much worse, even those who are the most gone cannot stand his company. Worst of all Aidis wears a short staff which was gifted to him by the Master, the very weapon which can imprison you in your mind and chain you to him." Stopping to sip, Lash moved to get more comfortable, then continued, "I didn't learn much during that time, but I did overhear a few things. There are or were four self-appointed Kings of Sirillia which serve the Master. Kurja you have already killed, Aidis is another. The Masters generals seem to operate independently from one another; that is how they can bring such suffering if you cut off one head, another rises twice as vicious." Lash's voice shook, belying the passion that she had for the topic, "The Master cares nought for us, his one true goal is to control the people and the land. I felt a deep hatred of us and on occasion, even jealously. Since the death of one of his Kings the Master has escalated his plans, taking his annoyance out upon the people of Sirillia, he has amassed an army to the northwest, and it has grown considerably in size." Before Morgan could ask a question borne out of sudden concern, Lash interjected, "I'm sorry, I don't know much about the army, I wish I did. I can tell you one thing, though. The Master will be taking his army to Tornbaer." Nodding resignation she let Lash continue with her sombre story, "My People are suffering, and our land is dying, those who won't fight are slaves, the free people of the desert now live chained and bound, one by one this land and its people are being put under his control. Tornbaer is the only hope for Sirillia's deliverance. We must stop him. His final goal is to walk among us; the only way that is possible is darkness to all. Please permit me to join you, Morgan, I have to make this right for my people."

In Lash's gaze she saw a determination that mirrored her own, with a firm nod she affirmed, "Ranger, see Lash to your cabin, you can bunk in with Marlo it's not like he uses his cabin. Lash, as soon as you are settled, I will come and see to your wounds." Amidst a myriad of maddening thoughts that were competing for her attention, she turned and executed a quickened stride, her office and contemplation called.

MORGAN WAS STILL TRYING to process her thoughts when she heard loud voices emanating from outside her office. She knew what the commotion was about from the distinct tone of Meena's voice. Morgan had been waiting for just such an occurrence since her crew discovered the existence of magic. Steeling herself, she stepped out into the verbal fray. Meena was in fine form; Ranger towered over her exuding calm and meekness amidst the jeering, "What kind of acolyte are you, you were useless in that fight," Meena hissed. Morgan steeped towards the fray and opened her mouth to speak, yet she was silenced by the sudden appearance of a little girl, who appeared seemingly out of thin air. Grabbing a few of

Ranger's fingers, the girl stared at Meena defiantly as if willing her to continue with her rant, stuck in the sheer oddness of the situation everyone froze. For moments, the only voice that could be heard, was that of Aiden who was in the washroom singing loudly and merrily about his looks.

"Can anyone else, see her?" Meena exclaimed, taking the words from out of her mouth. Ranger broke the spell by slowly bending down, when he was at the girls level he greeted her with a one-armed hug. The child who was about seven, had curly hair, dimples and grass stains upon her elbows, Morgan got a distinct impression, that calling her cute or adorable was a bad idea.

"This is the goddess Anene," said Ranger, looking anything but happy to be the centre of attention.

"He's under my protection" Anene announced, although her statement made her opinion clear, her solemn tone was ruined slightly by deepening dimples and an impish grin.

"This beats a talking bird and magical weapons any day," Marlo exclaimed, as always, he put into words what everyone was feeling.

Apparently graced with a short attention span, Anene saw Shev working at the ropes and materialised next to him, "What are you doing here old man, coming out of retirement?" She said impishly.

Not surprised by Anene's wistful behaviour, Shev shrugged and continued at his work.

"Carry on," Anene said cheekily, before flickering out of existence.

Blinking to ensure the child was gone, she turned to Ranger and asked, "Is she always like that?"

Uncomfortable under the attention Ranger lowered his gaze, "I have only just met her, so I couldn't say," He responded meekly.

Nodding, Morgan used the excuse to ask another question, "Ranger, what is the desert rose?"

Ranger pondered as if the question was complicated, then he responded haltingly, "I guess your closest title would be your King, but that's not quite accurate because the desert tribes have only ever bestowed the honour once before. Princess Lashima is the only person alive who can unite all of the people of Sirillia." When awareness of the importance of her new crew member dawned, she rushed away without a backward glance. It was again time to go into her office and practice on her dummy until worry, thoughts and fears were all quashed and soundly focused into sweat and determination. Sadly, that was not to be, as soon as she started swinging her staff, Anene popped into existence, infuriatingly plopping herself in the middle of her writing desk in a manner that was far from ladylike, feet together and knees splayed.

"I'm just going to roll with this," she announced, Ignoring the bum upon her papers because the child's face said she was well aware of her naughtiness.

"That's for the best, with your controlling tendencies," Anene replied with a wink. Anene spoke as if she had an intimate knowledge of one of the many questions knocking around in Morgan's head, "Although your Staff is the most powerful weapon that the Children made, there's a catch, it gives you what you need not what you want. My sister blessed that staff at a time when we freely walked among you."

Although Anene had given her more questions, she still felt uplifted by the imparted and overdue gift of knowledge, "I assume by your sister, you mean Amare, I had a feeling she wasn't done with me. Can you tell me why your family is always so vague with answers?" She asked respectfully.

"You can stop a child from going near the fire, but do they learn the lesson?" Anene responded dimples on display.

"What? That makes no sense, why would I let my children burn themselves, I need some answers to my questions, why can't you gods just be more hands-on?" She exclaimed, frustrated. She inwardly calmed herself when she realised, she was demanding answers from a goddess who choose to walk around with grass stains on her elbows; clearly, Anene had a hard time being serious about anything.

Anene rolled her eyes in a manner that implied that humans were so frustrating, then replied matter-of-factly "Because we made a promise to our father, that we would follow the rules, the repercussions of not doing such are why we are here today." Stopping to rest her face in her elbows in an entirely appealing manner, Anene continued, "I promise you Morgan, you will soon understand, just remember this, all four of the Master's Kings have weaknesses, Kurja's was vanity. Start by using the tools you were given; then you will gain understanding." At that, Anene blinked out of existence for an undisclosed amount of time. Morgan sighed, she was going to have to get used to not getting answers, something that infuriated no end, then it dawned on her, something Anene had said, actually made sense. Staff in hand she raced from her day room.

PROMISES OF YESTERDAY

*H*e was not surprised when Aidis materialized before him. Hatred was the only feeling he had for humans. Humans were a means to further his desires, means was of course, a fluid concept, Aidis was making up for his race's uselessness by serving him as only a worthless worm could. It took a considerable amount of concentration to use travelling magic so although he abhorred patience he waited until Aidis managed to spurt a string of words from his wormy maw, "Master, all is on track. Your army has moved into central Sirillia and camps at the edge of the desert. We will soon have the final piece. Morgan Jones will make up for taking away the ships that Fife Dallinger was to supply, by dying right before she finds out she will be supplying the ships that will be Tornbaer's downfall."

A growl in his throat silenced Aidis. Anyone else would be annihilated in an instant, Aidis however, was quick to make up for his mistake, stammering he continued, "Please Master allow me to continue to serve you. I was overzealous in my need to do your bidding. As you have requested, Morgan Jones will be captured and brought before you." A slight inclination of his head was all that was required for Aidis to leave his presence. The Masters hatred for all things human, was intimately known to all of his Kings, despite the fact there was little human left in them, they served him with equal parts of fear and loathing. Soon he would have his hands upon the very thorn that the other gods seemed to have taken a liking to, and nothing made him happier than knowing he could disrupt their plans. He still had not decided what he would do to her. One thing was sure, Morgan Jones would receive an eternity of suffering. The knowledge that all his plans were coming to fruition brought with it a sense of contentment. Although all that was left of him was molten metal, black fire and smoke, his black heart burned in foul desire.

DRIVEN by a vague idea of what if, Morgan's legs took her towards Castain and Aiden's cabin, thankfully Aiden was still in the washroom, she was glad not to have an observer for what she was about to do, although she wasn't quite sure what that was. She was still mulling over logistics when her presence caused Castain to stir. Eyes snapping open Castain mumbled as if in the middle of an animated conversation, "I am in awe of her, she is the youngest girl, but no one questions her decisions, everyone listens to and respects her, she has unwavering command." Castain continued to murmur, but she had stopped listening, it was evident that she was the topic of his ramblings. Feeling the weight of more unanswered questions upon already burdened shoulders, she sat beside him. It was as she was pondering what do next, that she realised she was over-thinking and had to act due to the sad fact that Castain was fading away before her. She gripped her staff in hand and placed it upon his chest, the anguished sound that came from him told her that something had worked. As his shout sounded inside her head, she was taken away from a suddenly spinning room towards darkness, the echo of his scream continued to fade to silence until the only thing that she could feel or see was oppressive gloom. Finally, when light flared before her, she was an observer to a series of scenes, it didn't take long for her to realise that the characters in the scenes, had a common denominator, Castain. She wasn't in her mind, she had been sucked into Castain's fevered remembering's of his worst memories. It was too late for surfacing uncertainty; she was now a spectator to misery. Understanding dawned that she needed to experience what was before her and although Morgan was unhappy about being led in such a way, she grudgingly set her mind to the task. Before her, young versions of Castain and her Mother in law Mira were in what looked to be a lover's quarrel. Castain was pleading desperately with Mira to make her understand something, he held her arms in a reassuring gesture, seemingly unaware of their placement, "You aren't listening to me, Mira. I can't ask you to wait for me," Castain begged.

"Then let me come with you, my parents are so angry they are threatening to send me to The Sisterhood of Amare. Please Castain, we can just run away from all of this." A hopeful expression accompanied Mira's plea.

Taking Mira's hands, Castain held, "You know I can't do that, you will eventually hate me for taking you away from your comfortable life and all that you love, I can't let you make those sacrifices for me."

A stubborn look suddenly graced, Mira's press lipped face, argumentative she said, "I won't let you go, don't do this, you hear me."

For a moment Castain said nothing, then he dropped her hands in finality, as he spoke Morgan felt despair and resignation as clearly as if they were her own, "I don't love you, you must do your duty, just like I have to do mine."

If she could escape from the pain, Castain felt she would have. Instead, she experienced Castain's chest constricting as he fought to breathe, turning away he placed one foot before the other, whispering under his breath, he said, "I will come back to you one day, my heart."

If she had a body, her hand would be firmly over her heart in a physical representation of overwhelming emotions. It wasn't just the sudden blur that told her time was flashing forward, seasons were suddenly blinking before her and just when she felt herself, getting disoriented, things slowed and finally stopped on another memory. At first, the scene was confusing, realisation soon dawned. The woman speaking to Castain at the bow of The Serpent was none other than her Mother. Cradled in her Mother's arms, a tiny babe, although she held the babe with gentle care and affection, Morgan knew she was the child. It was at that moment that she realised minus the fiery red hair; her Mother looked very similar to Mira. Swaying her arms slightly, to calm the child within the woman spoke, "The king is dead, you have no land, no family and no one knows you are a spy, if you came back now then you will be branded a traitor, we can't change what has happened, we have to play the cards that we have been dealt."

Placing a hand upon the babe, Castain resolutely replied, "listen, Leola, just because I must continue until I can safely ensure you and our child's safety, does not mean I have to like it." Realising that her Mother's name was Leola wasn't her only surprise, she was keenly aware that the endearment Castain felt for Leola, paled in comparison to that of Mira. More surprising still was the altogether different, but very intense love he had for the bundle in her Mother's arms, there was now no denying her father's love. What her

Mother said next sent a shock to Morgan's well-formed opinion's about her, "Look I have given up the life of a mercenary for Morgan. Don't go endangering us by staying any longer. I know you want to be her father, but we have to protect her, if they find out, they will use us to control you, that is what Kurja does. Please leave and don't come back unless it is safe for all of us."

"I will always protect you and Morgan no matter what, as you have asked I will keep my distance until you are safe," Castain said deflated. Accepting defeat, he kissed his child upon the forehead as only a parent could, watching Leola walk away, the intense feelings of loss and despair made her an interloper. Stuck with no way out, it was all she could do but hear him whisper under his breath, "I will come back one day, little one."

She continued to witness memories one after the other until finally, the scene shifted forward into a setting and characters that were familiar to her. Castain stood at the wheel of the Serpent speaking to none other than Marlo, they seemed well known to each other and Marlo was unloading in a typically animated way, "I know, I made a promise to you. Don't get grumpy with me Castain. It's not my fault that your daughter decided to storm a pirate ship and save herself. What do you want me to do at this stage, tell her you sent me, you are still a fugitive and a spy, what good would that do her, she would just go looking for you. You told me you didn't want her to be in danger, I will stay with her until my debt to you is paid, but don't take your grumpiness out on me." Castain felt deflated by Marlo's rant. It warmed her heart that despite the danger, he had tried to send her help. She could sense Castain's underlying anger and shock at finding out Leola had been shirking on her parental duties, worse still he felt a failure as a parent. Slamming his hand on the wheel Castain growled, "Marlo promise me, you will keep me updated, keep her out of danger." The fear Castain felt, wasn't just for Morgan it was for himself at the thought that there was no end to his misery, it was all he could do but look at the Brothel Beauty moored far away in the harbour and whisper under his breath, "I will come back one day Morgan, and you will know the truth."

Castain's words echoed, everything spun, and she was left only her father's thoughts to comfort her. Suddenly she found herself in familiar clouds. Walking towards her was none other than Amare. Amare's presence brought with it a feeling of safety and endearment. She did not have time to be surprised at her change of opinion towards the deity because Amare's words fired her towards awareness like a cannon-ball, "What was promised will be delivered."

She awoke acutely aware of all the things time and circumstance had stolen from her. The first thing that consciousness gifted her was Marlo's voice "What's happening here?" Looking up she felt a tear involuntarily form at the corner at her eye, the anguish and pain as each day he was pulled further and further away from his heart was still so fresh upon her senses. He thought of her each day, in the very same way she thought of her children. Marlo's voice again brought her out of reverie with its incessantness, "Morgan, are you ok? I walk in here after hearing Castain yell, and there you are unconscious on top of him, don't scare me like that, damn it!"

She was about to let Marlo in on her knowledge of his secret. Yet, she was silenced by a gaze that the now awake, Castain was giving her, affection shone in thankful eyes. Squirming under something entirely alien to her, she knew without a doubt that no one had ever loved her unconditionally in the way that he did. As if he had been aware of her presence in his remembering's he said with surety, "I will make sure you come home, or I will die trying." He ended the comment by gently accepting the tear from the corner of her eye, and he sat up in bed as if he could jump out of it in the next move.

"You can't promise that." She replied pointedly.

Smiling, Castain replied, "Fine then, I'm not leaving your side again, so as I have heard you say, if we can't come home, we will make them pay." She knew without looking that Marlo was standing there with his mouth agape. Although she understood why Marlo didn't tell her the truth, she needed to make him squirm, at least for a short while. She stood and walked away, feeling as if somehow so much of the world's problems had been taken from her, her step was lighter right up until she realised that the enemy now had something else to take.

WE ARE NOT IN TORNBAER ANYMORE

The rum fuelled fires compounded an already oppressive heat. She watched on dutifully, sweat glistening upon her brow. Morgan's sense of loss was heightened by the fact that her flighties were being cremated, laid to rest so far from home. Aroon walked between pyre and onlookers citing the traditional prayer of acceptance into Hanan's halls, when he was finished, those who knew the dead moved to say their goodbyes more intimately. Face typically impassive, inside she felt anything but calm, this part was never easy, even more so under increased responsibility. Reaching the main deck aboard the Tempest, she raised her arm. Marlo's deep voice boomed "FIRE" a round of cannon fire temporarily lit up an afternoon haze already brightened by lamplight and pyre. Cannon fire intended to salute the bravery of dead and live flighties alike, felt a token gesture on her burdened mind.

Soon after officers and esteemed visitors alike gathered in the wardroom for a post-funeral confab, one by one the officers gave her their reports, the effect was a gradual fall into sadness, then Marlo stood up, ducking his head he said decisively, "The good news, we are repaired and ready to go at a moment's notice, the bad, we have affixed temporary metal shielding to the cables and the hull is seventy-five per cent operational, for safety reasons we should stay out of the lower hold during flight until further notice." Turning to her with an expectant eyebrow raise, Marlo continued, "Give the word Captain and post lift away checks will commence."

It was better than she could have expected, "Lift away, as soon as you complete those checks," she replied, feeling heartened.

Impatience crept in and she directed her mind towards the heartening conversations around her. Lash who had already made herself at home had singled out Meena, diplomacy skills on display, she was employing a practised neutral tone to explain Ranger's plight, "That's what I'm saying. Ranger can't do magic because the only Magic in Sirillia requires some form of a link to the Master, that's why when Aidis reared his snakehead, his first act was to march anyone with the desired ability to Hero's End. Ranger's options were marching to serve or die. His choice was a brave one, not to mention if he is discovered alive, his family will be in grave danger."

Meena held her hand up, signalling the end of the conversation. She was about to come to Lash's aid, then to her surprise Meena looked towards a typically quiet Ranger and nodded, shyly he reciprocated the gesture. She knew Meena enough to see the motion was her way of saying sorry, thankful to Lash for defusing a growing situation and for having the good graces to quit while she was ahead, she continued to listen to those around her. Before long, another conversation had piqued her curiosity. Ranger who was slowly coming out of his shell seemed to be the most relaxed around Lash, amidst explaining her choice to run from responsibility Lash was animated, "I do not accept the title of

Desert Rose any longer Ranger. I felt I could do better by joining our people's fight, rather than be a useless figurehead hearing submission after submission and not being able to do anything about it."

Ranger who seemed more confident in her company interrupted, "Yes, but the title will always be yours, no matter what you do, it is your destiny." A shade of red hit Ranger's cheeks, and he stammered an apology, "I'm sorry, I understand why you felt the need to join the fight, you are courageous."

Lash placed a hand on Ranger's arm which spread the red across his face, smiling she reciprocated, "I could say the same for you, I heard the child goddess has taken a liking to you."

Ranger looker solemn, yet he looked at Lash with expressive eyes, "I know I can't match your skill with daggers and only know how to wield a pitchfork, but please permit me to serve you, If my life is all I can give than I will offer it."

Lash replied emphatically, "I accept your request and will hold you to that, but never again sell yourself short in my eyes."

Feeling an interloper, Morgan turned her attention towards Marlo who was amidst confirming Tanner had done the lift away checks to his exacting specifications. Noticing Marlo looking rather fatigued she opened her mouth to voice her concern, yet he silenced her with a pointed comment, "I'm worried about you, how are you dealing with the pressure?"

Smiling at the way Marlo had turned the tables on her, she replied in the typically deflective way in which he had taught, "Well, of course, the answer to that is plenty of bawdy songs, coffee, whisky, coffee with whisky and most importantly the care of friends."

Happy with the subpar answer, Marlo stopped any

further conversation by excusing himself to undertake the task of lifting the ship into the starlit desert sky. Before he could step over the threshold, she called out, "Don't forget a jacket, it will be cold out there." As Marlo left, she detected hidden meaning in his affirming gaze; then, he was gone, and other things pushed the fleeting thought into the forgotten distance.

MARLO FELT a sense of finality as the whistle rang into the eerie night. Relaxing, he stood at the wheel and started setting the leavers that sent residual heat into the mainmast tube. It was as Marlo was instinctively looking up to view the quality of the flame that he heard random sounds emanating from the Desert, best described as hideous screeching, one thing he knew for sure the sounds weren't coming from a friendly pack of desert bunnies. When the sounds got louder, he looked towards his stomach in the vain hope he was just starving, it was not to be however, as they got loud enough that the entire deck crew had stopped to peer into the darkness. Deciding he didn't want to meet the origin of the noises; he pulled another leaver to maximise the gas venting into the pocket. "MAN THE RAILS, READY THE CANNONS, THERE ARE SKELETONS ATTACKING," Aroon's forceful call caused him to involuntarily leap then subsequently panic.

Recovering quickly, he called for the release of the anchor ropes then mumbled under his breath, "We are not in Tornbaer anymore." Thankfully, there was enough stored heat to create lift and inch by inch the ship rose into the sky. The clang of swords hitting bone and the sight of Shev using a skeleton to knock others off the side of the ship made him grip the wheel in alarm. Fortunately, it was too late for their bony foes, because as soon as he had enough clearance, he engaged the rear mast tubes. The ship instantly picked up speed, and the added thrust brought with it a series of thudding noises that he assumed was the ship mowing down any skeletons unlucky enough to be in their way.

"How is it they can make those horrible noises without a voice box?" He heard Cheese exclaim, as the ship gracefully lifted away.

Aroon replied matter-of-factly, "That is nothing, one flipped the bird at us. Next, we will see dead seagulls fly." Cheese's only response was to grip his cutlass tighter and look suspiciously to the heavens.

Morgan chooses that moment to come barrelling onto the quarter deck, staff in hand with a I'm about to kick some arses look upon her face. He spoke as she skidded to a halt beside him, "Don't worry, I got this."

By the time she was at his side the tension had drained from her face, she said sternly, "Good to know Marlo, but you are gripping my wheel so hard, your damn giant hands are going to break it right off."

Smiling, he made an exaggerated effort to relax his hands, ruining her mock scorn with a hint of a grin, Morgan sheathed her staff and left him to his work. Instead of resting as was required she stopped to talk to her rattled crew. Sighing, he set himself to the task of operating the ship, he was always at his happiest when his handy work was running smoothly, and he was the Master of such. Making himself comfortable upon the comfy captain's chair, he had just readjusted his harness when a small child's voice spoke gently beside him, "We need to talk Marlo."

Although he was surprised to see Anene, he had expected a visit at some stage, "No we don't, we both know what is coming, and we both know there is no stopping it," He responded, adamant in his well thought out answer.

Sighing the little girl held her arms up in a simple gesture, when he grudgingly picked her up, she whispered gently into his ear, "I know that Marlo, but I'm still here aren't I." It became quickly apparent that no amount of alcohol or excessive work could soothe his warring mind, like Anene's gentle hug.

NOT USUALLY ONE for jumping at noises, Morgan was, however, a little on edge by her eerie surroundings. As if an ominous lodestone, the ship had turned to port when the climbing sun reflected on the column that was Hero's End, a short time after they had come across the random township in which she now stood. Although it wasn't their destination, aware that Sha could be secreted away in one of the houses she had quickly made the order to descend. The town around her was surreal by its very existence, desert tribes housed themselves in tents, not walls. Not the only one curious about their surroundings, Lash had insistently requested to be part of her landing party, the sheer look of wonderment upon her face as they wandered the streets told her the Desert Rose had no idea where they were. Their only welcoming party so far had been the odd child shyly peering from around a corner, although it seemed strange to her that a child should be in such an inhospitable place, she felt sure an adult would be found in due course. Central and protected from the elements by the houses that surrounded it was a meeting hall. Morgan reached her hand out to push upon the main hall door when she heard a child's giggle, turning to investigate her eyes stopped upon an elderly man walking towards them, palms up in a sign of submission he said, "You have come far strangers."

Although she got the feeling the man who spoke was more than he seemed, his demeanour was enough for her to sheath, and say, "I have no choice friend, I'm looking for a group of magic users, they may have come through here with a captive, a blond-haired gentleman with blue eyes."

The aged man looked to the tower in the distance and then met her gaze and said, "Welcome to Misery, there is a storm coming, you had better come with me." Unafraid, he walked past and continued into the hall, she hesitated only momentarily before following.

RED IN THE MORNING

$\mathcal{E}$verything ached, everything was darkness, everything was silent. Sha's stomach had long since given up on food, and his muscles were so weary, they would not allow him to crawl towards the lifegiving water upon the walls. He understood that he was rapidly spiralling downwards towards oblivion, but he just didn't care. He had been wandering blindly in an out of consciousness and was again ready to submit when he sensed rather than felt a presence beside him. At first, it manifested in the form of a distinct uplifting which grew with every moment. When his tired eyes finally set upon the little child, he assumed she was a byproduct of delirium, not that he cared, at that moment he relished in what she brought. Moving from standing before him the child sat beside then gently placed an arm upon him, "Well, this isn't the ray of sunshine I'm used to, why have you given up hope Asharn?" She asked, her voice soothing like water on burnt lips.

Surprising himself, he found the strength to croakily reply, "I'm thirsty, sore, tired, and so dehydrated I can't move, even I have limits."

Her smile disarmed his fears, and she said assuredly, "Let's do something about that shall we." As if he was a wounded animal, she moved her hand soothingly back and forward, her touch as light as a feather was enough to gift him instant freedom from pain, hunger and fear.

Grateful, he asked, "what is your name?" His recovered senses revealed an inner light was causing her to glow in the darkness.

A cheeky smile accompanied the child's upbeat words, "Anene at your disposal princeling. Now that you know me, I need you to promise something for me. When you feel this particular variety of hopelessness and despair again, you can repay me by preparing for the final battle." He had no idea to what she was referring but was so grateful he weakly nodded, then with a mocking bow and crooked smile she left. Thankfully Anene's uplifting presence lingered long past departure.

MORGAN HAD RIGHTLY THOUGHT that Misery was an exaggeratedly gloomy name for a town. Sadly, it was quick to show her it lived up to its name. Surrounding her was nearly fifty children of varying ages, none more than fifteen. Despite ready smiles, most seemed malnourished, in need of a hearty meal and clothed in rags. The older man who had met them had welcomed them into his home and introduced himself as Tenanu. His name had pulled a gasp out of a usually composed Lash, and he too seemed underfeed and weary. As the kids curiously inspected her seated group, she conversed with Tenanu about what brought such an odd group, to such a hopeless piece of the world. Like the children that surrounded her, his smile was readily available, "I, like these younglings have been brought here, me because of my knowledge of alchemy, them because they are orphans and have small but expendable hands." Tenanu explained, while handing her, his water skin. Noticing the alarmed look upon her face, he continued, "Don't worry, they made sure the only person on Mierma, left alive, that can make dragon fire is looked after."

She blinked in surprise, then politely took the water skin, after putting the pieces together, she asked, "So you were all brought here to make dragons fire for the master, why don't you just escape?"

Despite an undying sadness that seemed to lurk in his voice, Tenanu's reply was straightforward, "Where would we go, Morgan. Leviraan desert is very short on oases, then there are the troublesome skeletons, not to mention if I step out of line, they enjoy any excuse to harm the children."

She was still pondering Tenanu's depressing answer when Lash took the opportunity to blurt out a question, "Why on earth, of all people in the four deserts? I am a princess of a minor tribe, why would you name me the Desert Rose?" She was not surprised by the question Lash had been nervously fidgeting with her daggers ever since she had heard his name.

Tenanu looked at her, and calmly replied, "I didn't choose you, the gods did, I was just their messenger." Lash looked momentarily bewildered, then with subtle movements of her hands she made her daggers appear and disappear while contemplating his comment, the act drew a flurry of small onlookers. They emitted "Oh's" and "ahh's" as they pointed and stared in awe.

Aware of the passing time, she asked, "Why you, and why are you here in the middle of the desert?"

"They took it upon themselves to kill anyone else that knew how to make dragons fire. As to why we are here, I couldn't tell you," Tenanu said with sadness in his voice, it was at that moment that a small boy presumptuously walked up and plonked himself upon her lap, the gesture caused the other children to giggle at his brazen act.

Marlo who was waiting for just such an opening, inquisitively asked, "So if you are the only one who can make it, can you teach it to anyone?"

As if he had been waiting for that very question, Tenanu fished a piece of paper from his robes and handed it to Marlo. Marlo sat fish mouthed, Tenanu smiled and said. "Such a powerful weapon should not be just for the enemy, don't you agree?" Marlo's held the parchment as if it was going to disintegrate, then carefully placed it into his pocket.

She instinctively bounced the small boy upon her lap, feeling that the man before them knew more than he was letting on, she pointedly asked "Tenanu, can you tell us if a group come through here, like the one I mentioned earlier." The ready smile slipped from Tenanu's face, and after a long sigh, he said, "Yes they did come through here, their destination was Hero's End, that was over a week ago." He implored, "Don't go there, I beg you, it has to be a trap. Aidis is not afraid of anyone or anything, and although he is arrogant it is because he is a trickster, he will have a reason from drawing you to this place."

Disparaged by the confirmation of her fears, she took a moment to look at the smaller occupants in the room. There was evidence that Tenanu had tried his best to look after their welfare, a bandage here, a repaired rag there, it just wasn't enough. Meeting Tenanu's stare, she said with a conviction she did not quite feel, "We will be back, for all of you." Amidst the uplifting sounds of the children's glee, she stood, thoughts steadfast upon their impending mission's climax.

Soon after, they had completed hasty goodbyes, made it up the gangplank, and a well-oiled crew worked to get the ship lifted into the air. Morgan felt an overwhelming desire to run towards the fear that was lurking at the edges of her mind, standing at the bow, she stared fixedly towards the tower in the distance. As Gruth lifted the ship away, she turned her gaze to the waifs below, the sight of them exuberantly waving brought only guilt. As if reading her mind Castain spoke knowingly from beside her, "you are missing them, aren't you?"

Feeling like they were beyond the point of awkwardness, she replied openly, "yes, sometimes so badly, it hurts."

"Tell me about them?" He asked hesitantly.

Smiling, she brought her children's faces to mind, and replied, "Fareya is fierce and fearless, Gareth strong and silent, Darwain the joker, is always quick to laugh and boy is his laugh infectious, Fareya seems to be their leader." Turning her smile towards him, she let a rare display of unchained mirth forth, "I worry one day they will be troublesome, they are already a force to be reckoned with."

What he said next caused any remaining walls to drop, "I know you don't like to talk about this sort of stuff especially when we are amidst a voyage, but I would like to tell you. I wanted to send you to my parents as soon as I found out. Even though I didn't have the best upbringing, I still felt it would have been better than a brothel, Hautbas is so beautiful Morgan." Sighing he continued, "I haven't seen my parents since I left for Sirillia, my father reached out after he heard I had been pardoned, he is quite ill, much to my mother's chagrin he gifted me the lands and titles. I figured you could take the family to visit, besides you'll need a break once this is all over."

"Yes, that sounds like a good idea, after all, it seems we are always going from one crisis to another," She said bemusedly meeting his gaze, "You are still limping, how much pain are you in?" She lectured, pressing her lips together to hold back sudden emotion.

Meeting her gaze, he grimaced and replied frankly, "it seems not all wounds can be healed in such a manner." Grateful for an honest reply she turned her gaze back towards the tower looming in the distance.

Not long after as she pushed a message into the tube upon Aquila's leg, she gently stroked his back and politely said, "You carry an important message my friend, Leo needs to bring the kingdom together, fly safe, and if all goes well I will see you at home." His reply was an impassioned squawk which inferred that he would get the task done despite wind, rain, hunger, and a few other obstacles. After watching the majestic bird's last goodbye arc around the ship, she leaned against the rail and turned her gaze back to the desert below. The nearer the tower got the more secrets that seemed to appear as if her thoughts mirrored reality a surprising sight caused her to suck in air, beneath an expansive skeleton jutted out so far that no amount of shifting sands could attempt to hide it.

Lash spoke beside her as if her topic was commonplace, "That is a Great Lizard skeleton, it was said they roamed these lands freely during the early ages, no one knows what killed them, but there was a great battle in this desert, that much is obvious."

It was Brady who responded, "That is no lizard, lizards are little things that can fit in your hand, that is a nightmare, that thing better stay dead." Catching herself short of sounding panicked, she asserted, "I'm just saying." Smiling at Brady's narrowminded but understandable opinion, Morgan pondered upon the clear evidence that massive armies had fought significant and costly battles. There seemed to be so much from the early ages that was forgotten almost by design. Recently she had been unable to shake the feeling that the past was alive, just like the skeletons wandering the desert below.

Straightening her elbows, she pushed with her arms and released her hands from the rail. Tanner stood awkwardly on duty at the wheel, despite his intelligence he was not quite at home amidst the ship's controls. She was not surprised that Marlo had insisted Tanner be given more training, she knew Marlo enough to know he was about to impart a whole lot more responsibility. Feeling sorry for Tanner, Morgan had just shifted her gaze towards their destination when the feeling hit. It was as if a hand had reached into her chest and squeezed her heart without abandon. She found herself afraid to move fearful it would cause the excruciating pain to increase. The pain had only visited for milliseconds, and panic had already set in. With similar effectiveness it ebbed enabling her to move again, looking down she wasn't surprised to see Anene holding onto her leg, looking up with understanding in soft, expressive eyes. It was a second before she could talk, but when she could, she said in alarm, "What the heck, was that all about?"

"He is afraid of you if that happens again, just remember where your heart truly lies," The little goddess said squinting in the sun.

"Why would The Master be afraid of me, I am but one person," she said incredulously.

Anene's answer was typically and infuriatingly cryptic, "Because you symbolise what he fears, the worst wounds are those you cannot see, they are buried deep and protected by that which is seemingly harmless. That is what he is. A wound buried deep that we didn't see until it was too late."

Before she could reply, Tanner called, "Captain we are nearing cannon distance, what are your orders?"

Her reply was in a practised commanding tone, "Come to port and make a pass, all hands, man the cannons." As her orders bounced around the ship, she looked down to find Anene was gone. Feeling like she was fighting a battle on more than one front she went to find weapons and armour. If Aidis's was arrogant, she would choose her moment and exploit it by showing him, her special gift from the goddess Amare. It was high time to kick some arrogant, dark acolyte, arse.

PART TWO – HERO'S END

ALL DRESSED UP......

Fear of the unknown was gradually inundating a mind that ran on preciseness. Even after the third pass, Hero's End had revealed nothing, no nasty acolytes, no dead-eyed black cloaks, not even an untoward skeleton. Morgan's crew were all dressed up with no one to fight. Exacting in her standards, she found herself again inspecting the scene before her. Diligently at their posts, the crew shone in their new armour. Requisitioned by a well-intentioned Sha the hardened leather armour was accented by colourful panels, but Sha's version was strengthened with hundreds of tiny plates, crafted from Marlo's lightweight metal. The finished product ensured her crew resembled a version of the ship on which they stood; Sha's motivation had been to ensure her safety after his uncle had stabbed her. Her thoughts brought a pang of longing for his company, so she quickly shifted her focus back to the crew. Their weapons shone from polish, stone and sun and they impatiently shifted around in anticipation of a promised and long-awaited battle. She stopped herself from readjusting her sheathed staff; the resulting mental reprimand ensured that she stood in stoic defiance of the enemy.

Listening to her officers continue to chatter amongst themselves produced involuntary irritation, their ideas had flown back and forward long enough. It was time she made a decision. Holding her hand up to silence the voices, she said firmly, "We land just out of cannon distance. Castain, ready the landing party we discussed. Gruth you have the wheel, keep the ship taut against the anchor ropes we need to be able to lift away in an instant. Ready all cannon's to cover a hasty exit." As her words filtered through, her crew converted pent up energy into a rush to do her bidding and the usual butterflies mixed with her underlying fear adding strain to already frayed senses. Stopping herself from checking her weapons once more, she moved to await the gangplanks lowering. Her booted foot would be the first to meet sand.

The tower itself seemed to be made from the very sand upon which it sat, like an endlessly tall potter's chimney the higher it got, the smaller the circumference. Expecting anything, her crew's vast array of weapons was glinting in the sun on full display. As they stepped through the gates and into the central courtyard, empty arched windows, sand-stone and silence greeted them. Pressing her teeth together, she gripped her staff and stepped over the threshold of a suspiciously open entrance and into the impressive tower. After walking down the main hallway, her party entered the inner part of the building only to discover it was a dark and ominous copy of the outside. Aside from a row of rooms in-between, a hollow middle stretched the height of the building towards the roof far above, and the same arched windows eerily overlooked her party. Looking up, she surveyed to ensure there were no assailants before turning to assign tasks. Her commands halted mid-sentence, when her eyes stopped upon Marlo, towering over everyone he had a determined expression upon his face. For numerous reasons, it was never a good idea to have a Captain and First Officer in the same party. Although her expression changed only slightly, Marlo knew her well enough to know what she was conveying. Drawing his brows together Malo aimed a familiar I'm not amused look at her and said grumpily, "What, there could be a shit load of dragons fire here, and I'll be damned if I trust any of you, to know how to deal with the stuff safely!"

In no mood to argue, nor did she want to split her team to have him taken back to the ship, she simply sighed and turned her attention to other more controllable problems. Marlo had, after all, come prepared, his favourite quickfire crossbow was handy, and more than one grapple was affixed to his belt. Turning to Lash she motioned for her to step forward when she stood before her, she asked, "You mentioned, most of your time was spent above ground, but there were extensive tunnels below, we haven't meet any resistance of any kind, what would you suggest we do here?"

Lash's response was uttered with a concern laced voice, "This quiet is very worrying, it was always teeming with hundreds of people doing all manner of nefarious things. I didn't spend much time in the tunnels, but I'm positive that was where they held prisoners."

Looking above, Morgan grudgingly issued her orders, "Split into two groups. We search the tower first." Her instruction ensured their rear was protected when they entered the tunnels. She led her party through an agonisingly slow search, level by level room by room every passing moment was tinged with a growing sense of unease, continually pushing it down she forced herself to focus upon the task before her. Finally, the groups met to discuss their findings, the only notable discovery, seemed to be sporadic rooms filled with barrels of dragons fire. According to Marlo, the dragon's fire was stored in room's that faced the inside of the tower in water-cooled barrels for airflow and temperature control. As there were still no other signs of nefarious movement, she turned to Lash and asked, "There are a lot of tunnels around here, which one would you suggest we try first?"

Lash's apprehensive response was coupled with a firm grip of her daggers, white knuckles displayed her unease, "I would say the cells would be in the main tunnel to the east side, they regularly dragged prisoners in that direction." Most of the other tunnels were rarely used.

As her party entered the indicated tunnel, a lack of dust layers, dried blood and marks caused by what she assumed was prisoners being dragged away, indicated clear signs of recent use. A depressing thought that her foe had vacated and taken Sha with them pushed into her awareness. As the queasiness in her stomach worsened, she mentally scolded herself and continued to place one foot in front of the other; nothing could discourage her now, not even her ill-timed thoughts. The torches that lead them deeper were freshly lit, it was further confirmation of recent visitors, and she determinedly pushed onwards. Because the tunnel was so slim, her party had to walk two abreast and very quickly a downwards ramp revealed another level. Alarmingly this new level had only empty chambers, each of which provided dark unlit hiding places for assailants lying in wait, the anticlimactic result of which caused a gradual heightening of her stress levels. Onwards the agonising slog continued through a relatively straightforward tunnel system, and although there were side tunnels, they always choose the straight more well-travelled option. Each new level was heralded by a ramp and more chambers which popped up from either side. As the temperature slowly dropped, the only sounds not caused by her crew shuffling around her came from giant rats, she was not a fan of this example of her least favourite rodent, often they would race through the torchlight much too close for comfort. Already on edge, when Aiden pointedly spoke, those around him jumped in surprise, "One day you are as high as flying ships, the next you are stuck underground with giant rats." As the words came from his mouth, they bounced off the walls and just before they met the quiet, an answering sound could be heard deep in the bowels of the earth. Minute but audible, mainly because it must have made an almighty sound to be heard from such a great distance, she knew it wasn't good.

"Shit!" Marlo's exclamation mirrored her inner thoughts. Thankfully although the sound continued, it got no louder and slowly signs of life in the form of caverns filled with goods greeted them, a small but heartening sign of further tunnel use, At first they were filled with bags of grain or salted meat, then after that all manner of food stores occupied them, it was clear to her that they were stored for the army and judging by the types of food they were planning on a long campaign. Then the caverns presented them with other surprises in the form of gold, coins, jewels and other finery, like a spoilt child someone had hidden Sirillia's plundered loot as if to ensure that no one could enjoy them. Suddenly the torchlight stopped, leaving only darkness beyond. She halted momentarily, then after grabbing the nearest torch of the wall, she led her party into the unknown beyond, stopping only briefly to check for signs of footprints in the dust. Soon after, aside from depths and gloom, the torchlight greeted them with more caverns, these had been converted into holding cells. Forcing herself not to let excitement take over, she called for a thorough search of the area. At first, nothing but long-dead occupants greeted them, not allowing discouragement she diligently continued, then as she reached the last cell before another ramp she heard a shout. Realising she had, in fact, made the sound, she shoved her torch through the cell bars before her and let her eyes adjust to get a better view of the unfortunate looking occupant in the cell, lying on the dusty floor, forgotten and comforted only by the darkness, was Sha.

THE BARONESS OF AANLYIS was boorish on most occasions, none more so than this moment, Bella's stepmother had simply shown up after the engagement announcement, like a bad and very untimely smell. As far as Mira could tell when Bella was in the room, the Baroness spent most of her time demoralising her when she wasn't; anyone else was fair game. The whole affair had left her feeling increasingly protective of her soon to be daughter in law. As if watching a flower wilt, initially she had hoped Bella would rise from the oppression, instead the incessant campaign of destructive behaviour had left a shell before her eyes. It was now nearly a week into the Baroness's arrival, and as was expected of her, she had invited her son's betrothed's stepmother to the royal apartments. Ladies should also endeavour to read, do needle-work or simply contemplate in relative silence, infuriatingly however the Baroness was again talking in her direction in the abrupt manner in which she was now accustomed. Although she had a practised smile in place, regrettably she opened up her ears to the Baroness's nonsense, "I must again apologise for Ysabella's improper posture. At times she looks like one of my late husband's donkeys, I am not sure why she didn't get the good graces of a Vanglassen. I spent hours training her on such things." Seeing Bella flinch, told her volumes about the sort of training that was administered, on the Baroness harped. "I assure you however, what she lacks in manners she makes up for in child-rearing ability."

It was too much. Mira could hold her tongue no longer, politely as her mother had rightly taught her she held, "It seems unseemly to degrade a lady to the point where they are considered only good for procreation. I can assure you she has many fine qualities and is far superior to most of the maids at court. I must also say much more important than good graces; she saved my life-."

Before she could continue however she was interrupted by the sour-faced Baroness, "With all due respect your highness, I beg to differ, I mean the hours that I put in, were such a waste." Unable to fathom the uncouthness, she was shocked into silence.

Like a meek mouse transforming into a commanding lioness Bella finally and blissfully spoke. With no requirement to stand Bella met her stepmother's eye and said in the commanding tone of a Queen, "You will not speak to the Queen Mother and my soon to be Mother in law in such a fashion. Your behaviour has been, quite simply, ghastly. Apologise, or I will rescind your invitation, as is my right."

The Baroness's reply was in a shrill tone "How dare you, talk to me in such a manner."

Bella held the Baroness's gaze and continued in strength, "As you have said on more than one occasion, I learnt my manners from you, so if I am as bad as you have spent the last week saying then it is on you. I no longer require your acceptance." Mira could now see that despite losing many battles Bella knew how to win the war.

She was about to excuse herself to escape the tension when Leo strode in. Utterly oblivious to the atmosphere, Leo said confidently, "Good Morning Ladies, I was coming to see if Bella wanted to go for a ride with me." Before Bella's affirmative reply, a large Hanan eagle flew in the window. The Baroness's scream occurred in conjunction with Aquila landing upon Leo's shoulder.

Waiting for Leo to raise his arm so Aquila could scamper towards his hand, Leo took a small letter from the sheath upon his leg, and all went quiet in anticipation of the message it held. It was the look upon her son's face as he continued to read that sent worry into her bones.

"What is it, Leo?" Bella said, inquiring where she was afraid to ask.

Leo looked up to meet her eye, voice wavering in concern, he said, "It's from Morgan, she said there is a sizable army headed this way and because they may not make it back she needed to send us a warning."

Her heart hurt, she had no words, yet despite clear worry lines upon her face Bella spoke the words that she needed to hear, "I have faith in Morgan, my father used to say, only worry about the things you can control, so it seems like we have some preparations to make."

She was encouraged by Bella's words and the sight of her son drawing strength from his betrothed. Yes, she liked this girl very, very much.

CULMINATION

As soon as Marlo had the cell door opened Morgan sheathed her staff and ignored better judgement in her rush to reach Sha's side. Ignoring the myriad of thoughts competing for her attention, on hands and knees she desperately searched for an indicator he was alive. When no apparent signs presented themselves, she placed a hand over his heart. Thankfully senses tuned to her task were launched skyward when she heard Sha's week voice, "About time you got here." Overwhelmed, her throat closed, unable to speak she did what instinct necessitated and gently lifted her water skin to cracked lips. When he had finished sipping, he looked up with expressive blues and rasped in a familiar playful manner, "But seriously, it is about time you guys showed up, did you know they don't serve you duck a l'arlo here and they have a serious lack of cutlery."

Smiling, she gratefully fell into the typical banter, "Oh, you mean the one with the Lemon sauce?"

"What no, that's the chicken one." Sha re-joined sounding insanely casual.

Sighing in a deliberate and loud manner, she continued to

assess his injuries, and said, "You do, get yourself into these situations."

"You know, you like that about me," Sha said, sucking in air when she lifted his arm.

Finishing her assessment and happy that Sha's dehydration wasn't terminal she eased back into a familiar pattern of conversation, "Yes, but it would help if you showed a bit of sensitivity now and then. Always with the jokes, I was so worried." Worry silenced her mid-sentence. Sha leaned forward and placed his head upon her shoulder, aware that his arms could not hold her; she let him rest, meeting his gesture with her embrace. When Sha finally leaned back against the wall, she allowed him another sip, "Did you just sniff me?" She asked in amusement.

Sha replied with a familiar twinkle which had found its way back into his eyes, "You have no idea how many dreams I have had about your smell alone, not to mention the other dreams."

Meena, who stood protectively overhead, cleared her throat inferring they get a room. Ignoring Meena's feigned disapproval, she passed a small amount of dried meat across for Sha to suck on then said, "Well, well you are a romantic after all. It just took being locked up in a dungeon by evil, creepy, hooded, weirdos. I have been through hell, saving your arse. You could at least have mentioned how much muscle tone I have gained worrying for you."

"Your worry is my gain," Sha replied croakily, crooked smile affixed.

Allowing him another small sip, she said, "Always with the cockiness."

As if her comment had sent him from a dream to a nightmare, panic crossed Sha's features, and he said in alarm, "It's a trap, you had to have known that, why would you risk your lives and the lives of your crew for me?"

She did not have the chance to supply an uplifting reply; an untoward sound rent the air. The very same sound which they had heard in the distance, was now very much closer and it didn't sound like a bunch of maids clucking away happily, another more familiar sound followed the growling, guttural, wall vibrating screech, but not in a good way. Looking up to meet Meena's eye, she uttered the words in unison with her alarmed friend, "SKELETONS!" Ducking under Sha's arm, she hurriedly helped him rise. Flinching at his groan of pain, she said apologetically, "I'm sorry I know it hurts, but we must get you out of here right now, the skeletons are bad enough, so we don't want to know what is making that other noise." Her party protectively fell in around her, and she directed above the growing din, "Aroon take Sha and the centre. Meena and Aiden protect the rear. Taymah and Brady you are their back up. Keep swapping to save your energy." Relinquishing Sha to Aroon, she continued, "Castain you are with me at the front. Marlo, Lash back us up. Everyone else protects Sha."

With blurs of darkness, shadow and torchlight the tunnels that had previously taken forever to search flew past in a sudden activity to vacate them. Their first engagement with the skeletons was typically full of the crack of breaking bones and groaning noises that could only come from dead things. Pursued by a creature which seemed to vibrate the walls around them by its very movement through the passages, the deafening sounds of its screech's were alarming in their increasing nearness. The detail they were being pushed towards a trap was clearly evidenced by the fact that nothing attacked from the front. The timing was everything to Morgan's plan, so when she felt the warm energy growing from Meena's direction, she yelled "MEENA HOLD." Hoping Meena heard, she again pulled her focus forward where the sudden emptiness of the chambers around them signalled a nearness to the surface. Steeling herself for what could greet them, she gripped her staff and met her estranged father's eye, pulling strength for the subtle answering sword flick and nod, Castain's indication of readiness for the oncoming battle spurred her onwards.

Finally, her party stormed out of the tunnel and into the hallway beyond. The expected but unwanted sight of their welcoming party appeared before them. Standing in the main tunnel and blocking their exit was a few measly squads of Black Cloaks, their stances and swords indicated battle readiness. Standing at the front was the creature she assumed was Aidis. The Dark acolyte leader wore a cowl which hid what she assumed was a similar dead-eyed stare. More worrisome still, on Aidis's hands and lower face where she should have been able to see skin, instead amidst a backdrop of oily blackness something nefarious moved beneath as if it was ready at a moment's notice to wreak havoc upon the world. Yes, this man, was as far from being alive, as one could be.

Struck by a sudden fear that everything, she had fought so hard for, could be taken from her, she turned instinctively to check on Sha. Propped up by Aroon Sha was barely conscious and defenceless, heartened by a steely resolve she saw in Aroon's face and aware the culmination of their efforts was near. Determination took over, and she gripped her staff tightly. Slowly but surely her party was pushed by persistent skeletons into the exposed main room and towards Aidis's meeting party. The added room allowed Meena to use her ribbons, with a maniacal look upon her face, she sent pieces of Skeleton flying, at her side in a symbiotic dance Aiden efficiently despatched anything she missed. Those at the rear had scratches upon their bodies, the worst of which was a small gash upon Meena's face., The skeletons however were unarmed and easy to despatch, numerous they would eventually get through tired defences. Deciding it was time to refresh the rear, she opened her mouth to issue an order. Yet, her words were silenced by the appearance of more foe from above. Stepping into every arched window was two levels of Dark Acolytes. Menacingly they held darkness back from within their hands, as if waiting for their Kings command to reign death from above. Then as if to enforce the hopelessness of the situation, the oily drone of Aidis voice set her senses on edge, "well met Morgan Jones. It's about time you got here. it's impolite to keep your host waiting." Waiting for her to glance in his direction, Aidis continued, "Did you know. There are numerous tunnels around here, enough to flank someone if required."

Lifting one side of her mouth to convey cockiness and with a casualness, she did not feel, she replied, "Aww, a three-way, you shouldn't have, if I had of known you were this keen to meet me, I would have brought the dagger with your name engraved upon the blade." Seeing her comment brought annoyance to him, caused her no end of satisfaction.

Aidis mocked in response, "Ah self-assurance that's refreshing, although I wouldn't use that approach when you meet the Master, he has the worst temper and detests humans."

Unfortunately, her well-practised burn was drowned out by a deafening screech. Finally making its forceful entrance was the creature which had been pursuing from the rear. As the terrifying hulk which she could only assume was a great lizard came barrelling out of the tunnel, it then continued to skid like a dog upon marble, until it slammed into the opposite wall, the impact of which knocked most to the ground. As her party got back to their feet, debris and dust rained around them. The Lizard took a moment to shake its head and let out another ear-bleeding screech, like a creepy animated puzzle it remade itself before them. Placing one clawed foot upon the ground at a time, bones flew around until the lizard grew to the height of the room. Sensing the nearness of its prey, the creature proceeded to supply power into animated leg's and despite a lack of traction, on it continued thus, until it gained enough to execute a forceful charge. Turning back to meet what she could only assume was Aidis's smarmy gaze, she placed hands one over the other upon her staff and gently rested it on the ground before her. Closing her eyes Morgan let her senses take in all that was occurring around her. Just before the Lizard could impact with her crew, she firmly slammed her staff downwards into the ground, the resulting domed barrier was translucent and too much for the momentum fuelled rampaging Lizard. Headfirst her foe ploughed, collapsing upon contact in a spectacular fashion, suddenly devoid of foul life the Lizard's bones flew everywhere. On cue, Meena and Aiden activated their weapons the resulting brightness lit up the gloom. When she opened her eyes, she expected to see confirmation of a well-executed plan, instead she beheld a cruel smile. Uncomfortable understanding visited her when she recalled that Aidis's weakness stemmed from arrogance and her remembrance brought with it the understanding that she would not be taken alive.

CATCH ME IF YOU CAN

*A*idis's decidedly smug stare was stomach souring, chin to the air Morgan said defiantly, "Why don't you come a little closer, you would look good melted into a useless puddle of tar!"

Aidis waved a hand casually as if shooing away a fly, as a result the twin rows of acolytes above grew into countless levels of the same untoward onlookers all holding back orbs of darkness within their grasp. Allowing her time to process her new predicament Aidis slowly drew a black rod from his robes then moved his hands casually, spinning the rod in his grasp. She placed a mental barrier to block the fear that threatened to rise. Grasping her staff tightly, she switched her stance as if to say bring it on. When Aidis spoke, his unconcerned lecturing tone caused anger to flare anew, "Let's go through your choices shall we, let's say you use those oh so impressive weapons, even if you manage to get through the black cloaks before you, my troops above will focus their fire upon your ship. You can surrender now or be taken prisoner; either way, you are beaten." Stepping forward, clearly unconcerned with being in the vicinity of her barrier, Aidis continued, "Take your time to decide. I'm in no hurry. I have an impressive weapon of my own. The Master gifted me this staff, and it has since turned countless humans to his cause." Aidis made his point by bringing up the impossibly dark short staff, then with the same cruel smirk that she so desperately wanted to wipe off his face, he casually dragged it downwards upon the dome before him. Aidis's action caused sparks to fly from her shield and sent cold vibrations that ran up her arm and into her body. Her crew's response was to surround her, facing outwards they meet the enemy with menacing stares and polished steel. The vibration sat in her head like a stabbing interloper and hope waned with its unwanted arrival. Yet the answer was ingrained in her. Strength didn't just come from her weapon; it was brought about by her choices. Morgan chose not to give in into despair. Readying herself for a direct strike upon the being that dared stand in the way of her happiness, she kept the dome in place and brought her staff horizontal. Pulling outwards with her hands in opposite directions resulted in a bright light and two menacing-looking swords. Knowledge of the meaning of the glowing runes that burned brightly upon each gave her the heart to do what must come next.

It took a moment for her to realise that the pressure was Marlo gently grabbing her arm, he said something insistently into her ear, "When they follow, get everyone out of here as fast as you can." She was still processing Marlo's comment when he fired his grapple, then through levels of surprised acolytes he disappeared, all the while, he shouted mockingly, "CATCH ME IF YOU CAN." Marlo's yell was followed by comments about their mothers so unsavoury even a corpse would be offended.

Witnessing the open-mouthed surprised expression upon Aidis's features quickly followed by panic was poor comfort to what was happening above her, alarm lined Aidis's voice as he spluttered, "Get that man NOW, we need him for the master's plans."

The room descended into chaos, above rows of acolytes disappeared from windows in a panic to do Aidis's bidding. Aidis himself simply vanished before her eyes. Instinct kicked her to action and her crew followed her in slamming into the Black Cloaks who dared block their exit. Focusing on the singular thought to get back to the ship so she could rescue Marlo, she efficiently dispatched any before her. Suddenly an opening appeared, and the way was clear, racing through the courtyard and into the open, Marlo's gift of disorder ensured that the acolytes were too busy scrambling to do anything other than fire impotently towards her ship and party. Keeping the dome above she held back to help protect the rear. Finally, when the ship loomed before them, all momentum increased, until everyone, including Aroon who had smartly picked up Sha swiftly raced up the gangplank. Merging her swords, she gripped her staff tightly. Desperation grew with an incessant thought that they needed to get to Marlo before the Acolytes did. Meena's foot hitting the bottom of the gangplank signalled the last crewmember to board and taking in the unwelcome sight of energy bolts, Skeletons and Black Cloaks hurtling towards her she yelled in alarm, "LIFT AWAY, NOW!"

IT WAS NOT like he would ever be ready for such extreme decisions. Marlo had not known when he would need to execute his plan, so as he was lifted high into the tower, he was grumpy that things were happening so fast. In a quick and efficient switch, he reached the top of his first grapple, swung into an arched window and after aiming fired the second, the outcome of which was a quick boost high into the tower until he reached the level that he had chosen. Marlo had already gleaned that the acolytes would follow him. He was, after all, the sharpest tool in the workshop. Rushing in awareness of limited time before capture, Marlo swung into a window, dropped the grapple and got his bearings. Even an idiot could execute his plan; he should know he had worked with quite a few over the years, unfortunately, today, and under these circumstances, he was it.

With laden steps, Marlo strode into the desired room and picked up a barrel. Bringing the barrel high over his head, he felt silly for aiming so precisely then froze. Marlo had felt ready right up until this point. It was as he was psyching himself up that bringing seething fear in his wake Aidis appeared before him. His arms seemed to freeze in response to a straightforward word uttered by the King of acolytes, "Stop." He was still within his right mind, so despite the fact, there was no connection between his head and his muscles, he fought hard to regain control, a jerk of his arm told him he had nearly succeeded. Fear bloomed when Aidis stepped forward and said casually, "you, can stay right there until we can carefully place that barrel." As soon as Aidis's staff touched him, it was all over. Shunted by pain into the darkness, he found himself alone and powerless, disillusioned all he could think was, "*why did you have to hesitate you half breed idiot, why*." Then a voice which brought with it warmth spoke into his hopelessness "*Marlo Oryn, Son of Myrnia and Orin. It seems you are stuck in-between*" he could not see her, but in feeling her presence he knew it was Amare who spoke, she continued, "*Despite the choices of your forebears, you have chosen to walk in the light, despite your parentage you have chosen to care for others as if they were yours.*"

He was a bit short on time, so he rudely interrupted

"Look I don't have time for a replay of my life, I'm kind of busy here, are you going to help me out?"

He felt Amare's amusement, which didn't help with his irritability, "*Here all the time in the world is available to you, I was about to say that I will help you, but first I have to ask, are you sure you want to do this?*" Amare said, soothingly.

Resolve was readily available, and he responded in affirmation, "Yes, I am bloody sure, we both know this is my path, besides If you got to go, then it should be protecting the ones that mean most to you and in a fiery explosion."

"*Then I will reward you for your choices by granting your request. Remember, as always I am here,*" Amare said, her words brought warmth to his limbs and eventually gifted him the ability to open his eyes. Unfortunately, the first thing he saw was Aidis standing over him. The well-timed surprise upon the King of acolyte's face was answered by his release, as he threw the barrel. He had a moment to watch the trajectory and Aidis's suddenly panicked face then Amare embraced him, taking him away from fire and force, ever so gently saving him from the pain of death.

HOLDING a barrier in place while stepping backwards and dispatching skeletons, it was no wonder Morgan's muscles ached, and sweat dripped from her brow. She was listening intently to the sounds of the anchor ropes being sliced. She had thus far counted two crack's and in the fact she had more than enough time to make it to the top of the gangplank before lift away was reassuring. She was therefore not expecting to be deafened by the boom which rent the air, thrown from her feet by a wave of force her tailbone hit the gangplank causing a shock wave of its own. The sight of the tower or lack thereof brought disbelief in its wake. The only thing left of Hero's End seemed to be flying debris and a wave of fire which was thrusting angrily towards her. When she managed to get back up on unsteady feet, her ears were still ringing, so disorientation had already set in when the ground collapsed and the gangplank with it. Plummeting downwards towards a gaping maw she was surprised by her sudden lack of falling and glancing upwards brought the welcoming sight of Castain grasping her arm. Amidst an ominous hum, The Tempest now free of anchor ropes gently floated into the sky, in contrast to the chaos that was headed towards in the form of fire, groaning from the pain she brought her free arm up, pleased the staff was still held in it, she closed her eyes and produced the barrier anew, opening to the sight of orange hitting an imaginary wall, she focused on maintaining it as Castain hoisted her aboard. As the fire kissed the barrier like an eager lover, Gruth engaged the aft mast tubes, anxious to clear the ship from the endless orange sky. She continued to concentre holding back heat, fire and emotion and in her concentration she was oblivious. She was oblivious to her father's hand, resting gently upon her shoulder. She was oblivious to Meena's screams as she made to leap from the ship in a fit of despair. She was oblivious to Aiden grabbing Meena around the waist as she screamed in anguish and fought momentarily, then went limp against him. Finally, the ship cleared the fire, and she watched it recede backwards to what was now a gaping maw upon the desert landscape. Dropping the barrier gave shock a dwelling, and she used it like a warm blanket. Hardly feeling or hearing she barked orders, as the ship pulled away, quicker now, away from him. With only an endlessly burning hole left to mark his passing, she heard herself utter the order to head towards Misery. Her crew looked on in concern as she ignored a gentle question from Castain and stumbled towards her cabin. When she reached the safety of her cabin, she locked the door behind and dumbly walked towards her night room. Only after she had sighted the fitfully sleeping Sha, did she let the question slam into her mind, "Now what?" The only problem was, it brought with it all the emotion she had been holding back.

HERO'S END

er heart hurt. Uninvited and uncontrolled emotions mercilessly slammed into Morgan's already overloaded senses. The whisky should have somehow eased the torrent, But Marlo was dead. Silent and alone, warm tears moistened her face. She raised her glass to the air as if to salute Marlo and his bravery, the stupidity of her act adding to the maddening crowd, then because nothing made sense, she forcefully threw her glass against a wall and dumbly watched as the amber liquid dripped like her tears. As Morgan sunk to her knees, a cry of anguish borne of desperation escaped, and from knees, she unceremoniously dropped onto her rear. Realizing she still grasped her staff like it was a lifeline that should have magically fixed things, she threw it across the room. Her staff flew, as usual, it supplied what she needed, not what she wanted. The little goddess appeared amidst a flash caused by her staff connecting with the wall, barefooted and gentle she stood beside and spoke naught, "I didn't want any company," Morgan growled.

"Lucky for you I'm not any, my child," Anene replied gently.

The goddess's presence was soothing, and she laughed hysterically at the absurdity of such a comment coming from such a small example of a child. Laughter quickly turned into tears, tears turned in to sobbing, sobbing turned into inconsolable grief. Weeping, she sat in the middle of the floor unashamed in all her snotty-nosed, puffy-eyed glory. All the while, Anene rested her head upon Morgan's shoulder and cuddled until gradual subsidence and onwards until the gift of sleep was supplied by grief and exhaustion.

IT WAS late into the night when Morgan received an insistent knock on her door. The knock was accompanied by news of the ship's arrival at Misery. Duty was a good cover for grief, so she picked herself up off the floor and croakily called out to the message bringer in affirmation of her readiness. Taking a moment to wash her face, she quickly realized that no amount of water could make her look any less undone, so she gave up and opened her door. Meena stood at her threshold, with red-rimmed eyes matching her own. The sombre look upon Meena's face was tinged with concern and accompanied by coffee. Accepting the offering, an automatic smile of thanks sent bubbles of lurking guilt to the surface. Well-practised in compartmentalizing, she quickly excused herself and left her friend to attend to duty and detachment.

She had no smile for the orphans as they walked up the gangplank, their wonder-filled faces were lifted by the closeness to freedom, especially at the hands of such a contraption, indeed if Marlo's death was to mean something it was this. She dared herself to find some comfort in the fact that one by one they left their horrible lives behind them, alas still no respite from her grief. It was watching the scene that gave life to an idea. Consequently, as soon as it was confirmed their new visitors were settled on board, she called for a landing party and gave orders. A short while later, The Tempest was full of as much dragons fire as could be safety stored, as it hovered high above the desert town. Finding no enjoyment in the task at hand, she gave the order for the town below to be scorched in a manner that no desert sun could ever achieve. One by one barrels of dragons fire were dropped overboard until she was sure that it could never again be used to cause such strife. As the Tempest headed onwards long into the night, the sight of a deadly tower and a miserable town could be seen burning in their wake. When she was relieved, amidst her tired trudge back to her Cabin, she nearly walked right past Tanner who met her at the threshold, carefully holding a neatly tied stack of papers as if they were breakable. Morgan already knew the author of the documents, after accepting them, she let Tanner go. Dejected and alone, she went back to the lonely workshop. On top of the pile of papers was a letter in Marlo's hand. She contemplated putting the letter aside to read later, but he deserved better than her pain, so she made sure she was comfortable and with shaking hands read the agonizingly frank words.

DEAR MORGAN,

WELL, it seems the time is finally here, after hundreds of years, to lament my approaching demise. How you ask, am I writing this? My impending death is no surprise to me, I have recently begun to feel it is near, you see one gift which my family on my mother's side was given long ago, was the ability to know this with certainty. Kind of a buzz kill if I'm honest; I hear you ask, why didn't you say something? The answer to that is simple, my dear, I have long since learnt some things in life are written in the stars, and there is nothing even the great Morgan Jones can do about it. I had a choice to make and know this; I would make it again, no matter what the circumstances, I would always protect you and yours with my life. Besides you are so damn stubborn, you would have insisted on having it your way, and that stubborn streak gets more pronounced if your friends are in danger.

YOU BELLA and Meena are my only family, and so I would like you all to share my designs and of course the recipe for dragon's fire, they will give you an edge over any enemy and create a better future. I know enough to know; I will die because the enemy wants me and my designs, so please keep them safe. I also leave my journals stored in my room at Crewtown to Bella as I'm sure with her ability to read absolutely anything, the dryness won't be a burden to her.

FINALLY, I want to say that it has been an honour to serve at your side. For all my years those spent with you and your crew have been the most fulfilling. You have given my life a purpose, before I met you I was a leaf on a stream. I know I'm not the poetic type, but I think you will permit me this. I also know we have never spoken of this, but I love you like the daughter I never had. If you remember anything in this letter, remember this; you may be a Captain's bastard, but you are my Captain's bastard. Fly well and true like only you can, my Albatross.

YOUR FRIEND AND SECOND, Marlo Oryn

• • •

GRIEF VISITED her in an uncontrollable and chaotic manner. She had lost people before but never like this. Her mind was at war, and she had no control over which emotion would win in the battle for supremacy. She felt guilty for being alive when Marlo was dead, anger at him for leaving her without letting her know, sadness at missing his presence made worse by the fact everything reminded her of him. Castain chose that moment to knock lightly on her door. Unfortunately for Castain, the concern upon his features, made him an easy target for her frustration, after all, he could bear the weight of her anger, "WHY DIDN'T YOU TELL ME HE WAS A TARGET?" she yelled, angrily.

Castain's reply was measured and gentle, "It makes sense to me now, but I promise I didn't know-."

She cut him off, to continue with her anger fuelled interrogation, "Did you know he was into predicting his death?"

"I'm not sure what you mean?" Castain calmly replied, by now, an alarm was sounding in her head, but she continued anyway.

"What kind of spy are you, clearly a useless one." Her sarcastic retort caused guilt to finally override anger, closing eyes which suddenly threatened to leak, softly she apologized, "I'm sorry."

Indicating with her hand, she let Castain read the letter and continued to stare into the distance until she regained control. When he had finished, he soothed, "I'm sorry he felt he couldn't share this knowledge with us, but I have to be honest, I would have done the same as would everyone on board this ship." She wanted to disagree with his logic, but she had already let herself slide back into numbness, "I know better than anyone, it is difficult to be a Captain and grieve, but I am here for you when you are ready to talk." Castain continued as if he truly understood.

"Thank you, right now I need to be a Captain. When I do

take off my tricorne; you will be among the first I turn to." She replied numbly. With a nod, Castain reported and left her to troubling thoughts, most of which were about all the signs she missed that should have told her there was something wrong with Marlo.

After quickly checking on a vastly improved Sha she went to find Aroon, and before she had even spoken, she noticed the expression upon his face, "You know, what I am about to ask, don't you?" She said coolly.

Casually he replied, "Yes, you want me to be the new first officer instead of Gruth, I have one condition." Her reply was to raise an eyebrow, so he continued, "Nothing too cumbersome, I just want you to tell me well in advance what you have in store for our enemy, I know you are brewing something even now, aside from that, it would be an honour to take his place."

Nodding her agreement, she said, "Good, then your first act can be to run this ship while I get some damn sleep." Not bothering to wait for his reply, she quickly found herself securely enclosed in Sha's arms, and her thoughts had turned to the fact that she had selected her new first officer based on a desire to avenge Marlo's death. Before sleep claimed her, she couldn't help but wonder if the conflict to come would claim the lives of her friends and she would be left alone with only anger and darkness to keep her company.

The Tempest was a day out of Astrom, after using landmarks to gauge progress, Morgan pulled a leaver to slow the ship's headway through the sky, a night-time pass was preferential. Relaxing back into letting thoughts keep her company quickly she was lost in unconstructive deliberations.

An innocent question from Sha made her jump in surprise, "What is behind that dark, brooding expression?"

"I'm ok," she replied. She knew Sha well enough to know what he was asking.

Thankfully Sha didn't push. Instead, he did what he always did, asked her a question to divert her attention, "Soooo tell me, if Brady's name is Anita, why do we call her Brady."

Smiling to herself at the typical Shaism of trying to understand all her crews' nicknames, she was amidst an explanation when Tanner ran up in a huff. Waiting first for permission to speak, he blurted, "Captain, Shev is not on board this ship, nor was he part of the landing party at Misery." Raising her hand to silence Tanner before he could continue, she said pointedly, "Thank you for letting me know. Why don't you get some rest, don't think I haven't noticed, your lack of sleep, grab someone from the crew to help you." Nodding dumbly Tanner left bewildered at her lack of concern. Sighing her worry for Tanner's wellbeing was interrupted when Sha asked, "Wait what, we aren't talking about the Shev that lives at the Rose & Tickle's main Bar?" Nodding, she replied, "The very same, something tells me, he went to find some real adventure." Sha's reply was drowned out by a sudden idea forming. She was over worrying because the ones she loved were in danger.

As a dastardly plan formed the image of Marlo's stern face sprung into her mind, the picture reminding her once again that her heart could hurt in so many painful ways.

LIVE BY THE SWORD DIE BY THE FIERY EXPLOSION

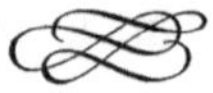

Expertly skulking through the streets of Astrom, her crew was appropriately decked out in dark clothes and sound dampening weapons, it wasn't appropriate however to be wearing such on an unseasonably cold night. Morgan found that working to keep her teeth from chattering took more effort than one would expect. Although she had disembarked more than a few hours ago, she was quickly losing her desire to be out under this particular sliver of a moon. Nevertheless, Morgan did not ask her crew to do anything she did not have the stomach to do. Truth be told this work suited her current disposition a little more than she cared to admit. Even though all intel had confirmed that Commander Orton and his men had been turned long ago, she couldn't quite shake the feeling that there could still be someone desperate to be set free from their mental prison. She had sent three squads out into the night to do the very same thing, seek and destroy any who manned and guarded the cannons and quietly dispatch any patrols along the way. Effortlessly finishing an unsuspecting guard, she helped to pour the readily available kegs of power upon the ground and waited for them to be doused, "Are you sure that is all of them on this side?" she whispered to Aiden.

She could not see Aiden's expression, yet she heard exasperation in his whispered reply, "Of course, I'm sure, they were all bloody shooting at us at the time, how could I forget."

She nodded absently in Aiden's direction, then embarrassingly aware that he couldn't see her affirmation called for a return to the ship. Abruptly and uninvited, anxiety visited. It was in the form of a sudden and unfounded fear that her crew and friends were in danger. Marlo's death had brought with it, such infuriating things and she wasn't about to let them sway her from duty, pushing it down she placed more power into her stride. She didn't have to like it, nor accept it, but she did have to admit that she had changed.

Anger and vengeance tasted sour in her mouth. It wasn't just the night-time skulduggery it was the fact that she had never issued a kill order unless someone's life was in danger, her usually perfect code was feeling rather shaky, one glance towards Sha gave reason. She reminded herself of her children and every other life that would be affected by the Master's plans, suddenly shaky ground firmed. Castain's purposeful limp up the gangplank signalled the final border, so she called for lift away and waited for the away team leaders to report. Heartened that the only injury was a bruised ego and a stubbed toe, she moved to the bow, to oversee her work first-hand.

She watched the scene from her perch at the bow, void of lamplight, the ship lurked the skies above Astrom, slowly and deliberately stalking its prey. Before the first barrel went overboard the streets were coming alive with surprised shouts. It was too late the impact of the barrels hit the garrison in a flare of brilliance. The dragon's fire exploded upon impact melting anything it touched, an instant reminder of the awesome power of the manmade substance. The walls melted, even where the ship lurked residual heat could be felt, and black smoke accompanied the screams of unsuspecting soldiers. The Tempest crew were not done, to the harbour they flew. Once there, she stood a witness as every sentinel class ship in the harbour was gifted by barrel after barrel of dragons fire. Only when the carnage claimed a score of Fisherman's vessels did she allow sadness. Still, she watched, and before long all that was left of the once impressive fleet was bright orange lines burning as they sunk to the bottom of the harbour. Yes, if Commander Orton were still alive, he would have no weapons to use against the kingdom, and this would provide a considerable setback for the Master and his nefarious plans.

She continued to watch and witness the horrible sights and sounds long after giving the order to head home. Castain walked up to her clothed in darkness fresh from night-time blood spilling. He said nought. "I know what you are thinking, this isn't me," she said, dropping her guard.

"No, I was thinking that I never wanted this life for you," Castain replied sombrely, staring into the distance.

"You think I choose this?" She exclaimed in surprise.

Castain was silent, yet just when she was feeling an edge of annoyance, he uttered deliberately measured words, "Don't misunderstand my meaning. I could never judge you. I just meant that I understand what you are going through. Just remember, no matter how hard this is, accept feelings of guilt for what they are. Your guilt is what sets you apart from your enemy," cloaked in the darkness she nodded dumbly, allowing him to continue, "Morgan, we often think, if we could just change everything today, we will be able to control tomorrow. That is not how life works, take it from someone who knows, it's hard making decisions that align with a desire for vengeance, and you will always second guess your-self because you are good."

"How do you know me so well?" She said, amazed.

Although she couldn't see it, she heard Castain's smile, in his pointed response, "Because you are so much like me at the same age, but even better, you have your mother's passion and drive."

Suddenly feeling resentful she growled in, "Don't, talk about her, I am, nor will I ever be like her."

Castain let out an audible sigh, turning to stare at the moon he spoke gently as if afraid of her reaction, "Morgan, there is so much you don't know about her, but that is not my story to tell, just remember I will always have your back no matter what." At that Castain, limped away, leaving her under a lonely moon, with only racing thoughts to keep her company. Suddenly remembering where she was, she raised her barriers and sat in silence. Silence mocked her, suddenly her mind was so full of unrest she needed relief; It was time to train. Morgan was acutely aware that she was deflecting, it was time to expend enough energy to bring on exhaustion, only then could she belay nightmares of screams and name-less faces.

AIDEN WAS A BEGGAR FOR PUNISHMENT, or at least he thought so at this particular point in time. He could no longer stand to watch as Meena continued to exhaust herself in this manner, infuriatingly and unlike the rest of the crew she had chosen to ignore numerous commands from Morgan requesting that she rest or eat. Sometimes she had even pretended to follow an order, then relying on Morgan's busyness had done the opposite. Stepping forward he brought his palms up in submission. He knew he was taking his life into his hands yet it couldn't be helped, anything was better than the torture of watching Meena fade. Keeping his hands up, he slowly advanced in a direct but careful manner, step by step he got closer until just before he stepped into a flurry of sword strikes, thankfully Meena let up. Stopping with a sweep that went very close to the left side of his head. Sweat dripped from her furrowed brow, and she stood there looking lost and confused, "what do you want?" She growled, he knew her well enough by now to detect a lack of fervour.

After slowly lowering his hands, fearful of being silenced he blurted out his concerns, "I just wanted to see if you were ok. I know you aren't the sort to talk about that, I just have to ask Meena." First ensuring, no swords struck out in his direction, he continued, "I have watched you at it for days, you don't eat or sleep, all you do is this, and at the risk of getting gutted, I'm worried about you."

It was as he realised that he meant what he said that Meena's half-hearted attempt at sarcasm met his ears, "Wait, the most self-absorbed person on this ship is worried about me, whatever will I do!"

He was pretty sure that despite her tone, she was noncommittal and her comment lacked her usual fire, so he re-joined, "Look, I just came over here to say, I'm here for you if you need me."

He was trying to elaborate further when his groupies walked up and in a very uncouth manner, watched him stumbling over his words, thankfully they did not giggle. Exasperated, he noticed Meena's raised eyebrow and said, "Ok, I'm going, please remember what I said." Slowly and deliberately, he brought his palms up again, and backed away, all the while studying her features. What he saw there made him feel something infuriating and unfamiliar. Thereupon her beautiful face was a slight hint of a smile. It took him a while to place the strange feeling. Pondering to himself that easing her suffering brought him happiness, he stumbled upon an uncomfortable truth. He was besotted, confused he walked around in a daze, nearly bumping into a few sailors, on his new quest to find Castain.

FINALLY, with some actual sleep under her belt and despite the lurkers in her dreams, Morgan was feeling refreshed. Enjoying Sha's company in the morning sun, she was reminded by his demeanour that he was almost back to full swing. Harnessed up beside her, Sha was prattling on about his favourite subject, her crew, "So as I was saying Laiken's name is Murray, I mean who calls a baby Murray." In his most masculine voice he pantomimed holding out a babe and said with feigned contempt "Esmeralda, would you change Murray's diaper it smells like a rat died-"

Brought out of her pondering by his comment, despite the fact her heart wasn't in it she proceeded to berate him, "Sha, you can't just say stuff like that, especially on a ship full of ex pirates, someone could take offence."

"Gee I'm sorry. To my defence, I was only repeating what he was saying about himself," Sha replied, sounding downtrodden his smile slipped.

Feeling bad, she downgraded her scorn and replied gently, "We are only responsible for our actions Sha, not other people's."

She was already feeling out of sorts when in a flash, the little goddess blinked into existence. Infuriatingly Anene sat with bottom to rail casually resting elbows on knees as if she cared nought for the effect that it had on Morgan's already frayed nerves. As if she had been present during the conversation, Anene said matter-of-factly, "Don't feel bad Sha, she's only lecturing you, because she has lived so many lives."

The smile slipped off her face when she realised to whom Anene was referring. To stave off warring thoughts she noticed Sha's bewildered reaction and gave introductions, "Sha, this is Anene, she is the goddess of many things, but it seems most of all, our hearts."

Smiling at the praise, the little goddess purred, "Well, you do know how to impart a compliment."

Leaping up onto her feet, Anene aimed a warm smile in Sha's direction and proceeded to walk backwards and forwards upon the rail, "Wait, I know you, you saved my life!" Sha blurted.

Surprised by Sha's comment, she looked to the goddess for affirmation. Instead, all she got was the smile.

Sha chose that moment to blurt out a string of nonsense as if he was able to completely ignore the fact that the goddess was walking with arms outstretched, bending at the knee every so often to dip a foot below the rail, "You are seriously adorable. Your voice is so cute, and the curls. Even better the smell of grass. How on this earth am I supposed to take you seriously?"

That did it finally Anene stopped her infuriating walk, leaping down from the rail she placed hands on hips and advanced towards Sha. Sha was pushed backwards with every undeniably adorable word, "how does one get a little respect around here. I prefer if you don't call me adorable, and seriously the c-word."

Anene's suddenly stern demeanour was unfortunately ruined in the way she stamped her foot for effect after every point. By now Sha had reached the end of his tether and looked rather panicked. Knowing Anene well enough by now to defuse the situation, she held her arms wide and entreated, "I'm sorry for Sha's exuberance, how about I make it up to you with a hug, come on now, you know you won't get that offer from me often and in front of my crew nonetheless."

Anene's face lit up and much to her crew's mirth Morgan was soundly crash tackled by an exuberant goddess. Feeling lighter than she had in a long time. She thought to herself "Yes, with a set plan and a goddess available to hug, all would be well." After Anene had left to find Ranger who she announced was her favourite, Sha gently asked her an impossible question, "Are we done with vengeance, for now? I, for one, would like to know what else you are planning."

She feigned a thoughtful expression, then replied, "Yes, we are done for now, when I know my next move you will be the first to know," Just like that, the lies had begun.

SOME THINGS NEVER CHANGE

$\mathcal{D}$uty was so dull he much preferred a good campaign, the stray thought made him cringe. Images flashed into his head, he mentally scolded himself and reaffirmed his love for boredom in all its forms. His compatriot poked him, then pulled him to awareness with a comment, "Oi Bob, can you see that? It's a ship and it could only be one, considering its flying."

"It's your turn, Gary," He said, adding a shrug to feign indifference.

Gary went on the counteroffensive, "No, that's not true at all. I helped the sergeant drill that hopeless soldier."

Despite the fact Gary had a point, Bob felt he held the fool in his hands, so he countered, "You told me last week after I got you that date with the candlestick makers daughter, you would do anything for me, remember."

Uplifted by the fact that he knew he had a point, he watched as Gary trudged away grumbling to himself. Yes, the day was looking up, Morgan Jones had arrived which meant Marlo would be available for stories and drinks aplenty.

· · ·

A CALM END to a chaotic mission, The Tempest soared into Bastien and gently kissed the water of the bay before she made her final approach into the Royal Docks. Morgan was surprised to see a sizeable and colourful crowd waiting for her to disembark. When gangplank hit dock, she hesitated at the top feeling underdressed, she was among the few who could bear weapons and armour in the royal presence, and she wore them proudly, yet her eye took in a sickening display of weapons, colour and excess. Nearly every noble from Tornbaer seemed to be staring and whispering in her direction, in response Morgan stoically stepped forward and met the pomp with her defiant answer to such, indifference. At the base of the plank was a sight which nearly caused her façade to crack, there Leo confidently waited, on his arm a porcelain doll, although she knew better than to assume Bella was breakable. She proceeded to descend, staff in one hand, Sha on the opposite arm, a deliberate reminder to those below, of her status. She was about to step off the end of the gangplank when she froze, Sha seemed to read her mind and leaned in to whisper, "It's ok, we just need to make it to the royal apartments, and we can unwind. Come on, let us get this over with." Gripping Sha's arm, she grudgingly let herself be led until she stood in front of Leo.

Leo had a smile that conveyed his welcome and seeing the glint in his eye made her feel secure in the knowledge that she was at her home away from home, meeting Bella's gaze she inclined her head in a greeting that spoke volumes. As decorum dictated Leo spoke first, his hearty greeting rang out, cutting through the whispers, "Protector, it's a pleasure as always. I can't begin to tell you how happy I am to see my brother safe." Leo momentarily lost composure then as if remembering the company he was in continued, "If Bob hadn't have seen you from the main balcony, I wouldn't have had an excuse to call a much-needed break from our talks.

You will need to give your account at the royal assembly, of course." Thankfully, Leo read her expression, then blissfully as if reading her mind, continued, "ah, of course, that doesn't have to be today, I will extend the break until tomorrow, so you can unwind and rest."

Bowing her head in thanks, she opened her mouth to respond when she noticed Leo's attention pulled by something behind her. Ascending to a wave of murmurs, Lash was dressed in a stunning example of traditional desert garb, the shimmering dark layers of sheer cloth seemed to have a life of its own. Like a true princess, Lash floated towards the waiting crowd. The fact Lash was on Ranger's arm only seemed to make her stand out even more. Unfortunately, it wasn't just her beauty that caused a stir among the intolerant crowd. It was also the fact that Lash and Ranger's sun-kissed skin marked them as far from the pale pallor, of a Bastien dandy. It seemed to her that these nobles had no idea who their true enemy was. Sighing, she took the opportunity to make introductions, "May I present, Lashima Shllashan, Princess of the Storm, hailing from the Reshda Tribe and more importantly, The Desert Rose."

Leo looked like he was trying to put a puzzle piece together, then Bella spoke politely from his arm, "Your Majesty, the Title Desert Rose is Sirillia's female equivalent of yours."

Leo recovered quickly, "My Lady, may I offer my arm, to give introductions?" He said politely turning towards Bella.

"Of course, sire," Bella said regally, she released Leo's arm and executed a graceful bow. It gave Morgan a warm feeling inside, to see how Bella shone like a rose among thorns. As decorum required Leo stepped forward, to offer his arm to Lash, Lash lightly rested her arm atop and allowed herself to be led towards the nobles who were all pretending to look uninterested, although were anything but. It was as she was pondering that Lash needed no protection due to the number of daggers she had stashed, that Hector stepped into her view. Morgan had met Hector during the long and arduous procession that was her wedding, and as usual his no-nonsense nature reminded her of why she liked him.

"About time you got here, I could do with a decent sparring partner. I've had to put up with some pretty piss poor competition lately," Hector said matter-of-factly.

Slipping into typical banter, she replied, "Sounds perfect, I don't often get the chance to practise, on sword and shield techniques, have you stopped trying to chop down trees with that double-edged blade of yours?"

He raised an eyebrow at her comment, then gruffly replied, "What's the point in having a sword, if you can't cut a limb off with every stroke." Moving to stand protectively beside Sha, Hector conversed in the same familiar fashion all the while surveying the scene around him. She knew Hector was on edge, yet knowing this wasn't the time or place she pressed her teeth together, gripped her staff and reluctantly stepped forward. Luckily as Leo Introduced Lash to the waiting procession, she was reminded of their names and titles. Morgan was also reminded that before her, was a bunch of pompous, snotty-nosed, stuck up, fake excuses for humans, yes, some things never changed. The second-highest ranked family and the first in Leo's introductions was the Bonnards. The family of which Mira hailed, they ruled over the duchy of Dulcea, from an excessively large and spread out castle to the north known as The Gatehouse, appropriately named such because it had a lot of gates. She watched as Leo introduced Lash to the Duke of Dulcea, Kritchner Debou Bonnard like most of his peers, stuck his nose in the air. The Duke's retinue surrounded him, dressed in typical Northern fashion, their bright coloured clothes were supposed to represent the flower gardens of the gatehouse, but she found the whole effect quite garish.

It was as she was blinking from the brightness that she noticed a slender, wiry man seemingly appear from the shadows beside the Duke. Dressed all in dark leather, he looked way too much like a black cloak for her comfort, thankfully the fact his eyes continuously scanned the crowd for hidden dangers confirmed he was in fact, the Duke's Master of the sword as was introduced. After she had made niceties with the Duke, she made to move onwards. Before she could take a step, the sharp features of the darkly dressed man met her, hunching slightly to be polite he held out his hand in a typical solder greeting, and said, "Ajaib Sarestra Gatehouse Master of the Sword, at your service."

She did not sense an air of rudeness, but because Ajaib was an unknown element, she shook his hand and replied, "Well met Ajaib, Morgan Jones Protector of this realm, may I inquire why you are master of the sword when your preferred weapon is the spear."

Ajaib looked at her, hiding surprise behind narrowing eyes. Ajaib's eyes moved to the tell-tale callouses on his hands, and he said, "It seems your reputation isn't exaggerated. I hail from the Craggy Isles as you have probably already suspected. I would like to test said reputation and have a match against you."

His request was respectful even for a sheepherder. Nonetheless, she wasn't one to openly display her skills purely for curiosity and was about to comment on such, when Meena spoke belligerently from behind, "Well, I hope you know how to stick something with your stick, tall man."

Worried about a diplomatic incident, Morgan made to politely exit, when the Duke of Dulcea snobbishly interjected, "He has saved my life on more than one occasion, I would put my money on him over you any day."

The Duke's comment was said down the nose and directed at her, despite the origin of the insult, with a slight incline of her head she politely replied, "Unlike in the North, we don't bet on bouts blood sport is frowned on here, good day to you."

Not waiting for a reply she continued onwards, all the while wishing for the string of endless faces to end, soon after the southern nobles flew by in more muted colours, it wasn't just because Bella was from the south that she much preferred their manners. However, that may have been because their opinions were hidden behind polite gestures and niceties. She felt uplifted by the sight of the crowd thinning. That was until she met Bella's step-Mother, she was all hard angles and open disdain. The woman wasn't even that important, but was overtly asking for a face slap. Thankfully Meena didn't lash out, and after leaving the abrasive harpy behind, things got a little better. Head Chief Freeholme was the leader of the Plains Herder's, Guijui Freeholme and his entourage were her kind of people. They were adorned in sturdy riding cloaks and tan leather armour, with flared skirts, this, of course, was so they could ride and move upon their warhorses with ease. Morgan had been captured as a child by stories of the Plains herd, and she would escape reality by daydreaming of her adventures on the Plains. It was said that you were not an adult in the Plains unless you could throw a spear into a man at a gallop, although they did not spend much time at court, she was not surprised by their appearance Plains herders could be depended on when there was a war to be had. Like a breath of polished leather, they were exposed and honest in their opinions. Regrettably she had to move onwards, and so the faces continued to pass until finally the sea of nobles parted and there waiting, was a freshly saddled horse and a short ride to the Citadel.

A beaming Piper greeted her as her horse's hooves met

the courtyard and she noticed Mira let her frown slip when she saw her middle child. After Mira had finished inspecting Sha for dents, she strode purposefully towards Morgan, causing her to tense involuntarily. Yet before Morgan knew it, she was embraced in a genuine perfumed hug. Thinking to herself, this must be what it feels like to have a mother, it was all she could do but awkwardly return the gesture. After her compose was again established, Mira said gracefully, "Thank you for bringing him home safely." Before she could respond, Mira excused herself abruptly, with a tear in the corner of her eye she hurried away to ensure the kitchen staff had the nightly banquet organised and all was right for their stay. After sending a runner towards Denza to warn of her crew's impending and thirsty arrival, she followed her friends into the Citadel and towards the Royal Apartments.

As a group, they walked the Long Hall making small talk and enjoying the familiarity of the company of friends, Bella however, couldn't wait to impart pressing news. Bella grabbed her and Meena's arms and pulled in the direction of a quiet alcove. Leo, Hector, Aiden and Sha seemed to get the idea instantly, standing in a row with their backs to the girls, they politely conversed with one another, shielding them from the curious onlookers who continued to trail past. All three of them talked at once in a cacophony of noise this happened a few times until realising what Bella was saying she held up her hand sharply and motioned for her to speak. Hesitant after learning she was the centre of attention, yet Bella found her voice, "please don't go off somewhere that dangerous without me again. Knowing I couldn't be there to have your backs was unbearable, I pulled you both in here because I need to give you some important news."

With every polite word Bella spoke, Morgan felt the heavy mantle of duty and expectation fall from her shoul-ders, and she fell into the peaceful comfort that was her sister's company. Yes, they truly were the sisters of her heart. Meena playfully interjected before Bella could finish her request, "Yes, we know you missed us, we missed you too."

Bella smiled shyly and said, "well yes, of course, I missed you, but that wasn't-"

As Meena had already fallen into a familiar pattern, smile affixed, she again interjected, "Eww Bella, are you pregnant?"

Bella went red, which was her version of scandalised, then after seeing Meena's smile she continued, "ah, no that's not what I was going to say-"

Again, she was interrupted, this time Meena faked a scandalised tone, "oh no, so you and Leo have had a huge fight, and now you have to go to a nunnery, to live out your days in shame." Adding a backwards hand over the forehead Meena feigned a swoon.

"You are in a good mood Meena anyone would think you are in love or something," Bella said amidst her giggles with no idea how close she was to the truth.

Meena's face suddenly lost its smile, and waylaying a harsh remark she interjected sternly, "Gee Meena, can't we just, let her speak."

Meena mouth was still closing as Bella blurted two words. "I'm engaged."

Still, in a playful mood Meena responded casually, "Oh, I see now, well that Hector fella's, pretty easy on the eye, and he's built like a Gatehouse cage fighter."

Although they all knew who Bella was engaged to, like the young lady's they were, the randomness that was Meena's jovial remark, sent them all, into fits of long-overdue giggles. When they finally regained composure, Meena pertly enquired, "Soooo, who's the main maid?"

"Both of you." Replied Bella, Beaming from ear to ear.

"Oh yeah, time to kick some arse," Meena said with ferocity. For a split-second Morgan was confused by Meena's comment, then she remembered what had occurred during her pre-wedding celebrations and laughed along with her friends. Although they still had their backs turned, the men seemed to be amidst exchanging glances that inferred these ladies were a rare and crazy breed.

She abruptly stopped laughing, when she felt the guilt that maddeningly clawed to the surface, Bella, who was sensitive to such, spoke concern laced words, "Morgan, what is it? What is wrong?"

Words failed her, how was it that she could shift from joy to despair just by thinking of the newly departed. It was as she continued to fight a battle to regain composure, that Bella cried out in alarm, "Wait, where is Marlo?"

Sha shifted uncomfortably on the spot, thankfully along with the other men he maintained cover, their backs the staunch privacy that was suddenly required, allowed them to be for each other what they had always been, sisters in everything.

When the gang stepped into the main parlour, all decorum went out the window. Morgan's senses were assaulted by varying conversations, some were about catching up, others were about comforting each other, and to her amusement, one was about reconciliation. Framed by the enormous doors that lead to the main balcony, were Mira and Castain, oblivious to the world around them. Their heads pressed together, the smouldering intensity in their gazes caused any who glanced in their direction to grin. After mentally berating herself for staring, Morgan looked around the room for Leo, already tired from a lack of sleep and prolonged harbour greetings, she felt an overwhelming desire to report then relax. Unfortunately, it was when she nearly stood before him, that Morgan realised he was comforting a saddened Bella, suddenly feeling an interloper to an intimate conversation she made to inch away. Yet, Leo called out insistently, "Wait, Morgan, I need to hear your report," Hesitating, Leo's features softened, and he added gently, "I need to hear, how this happened."

Nodding she swallowed then stepped forward, she began

her story at receiving a letter in Crewtown and ended her story at sinking ships. She hesitated when she had to articulate how Marlo died. Thankfully, Morgan made it through her report relatively unscathed and then proceeded to wait patiently for Leo's questions. Instead, Leo sat there with a thoughtful look upon his face. While Morgan waited for Leo's input, she took in the sights of the room. It heartened her to see Lash conversing with Hector as Ranger watched on. Ranger's height ensured he stood out like a sore thumb. It was nice to see her new friends treated like members of the gang. Suddenly Leo's question took her by surprise, "You have changed, haven't you?"

It was a yes or no question, yet she surprised herself by bitterly over-sharing, "I have always taken everything in my stride. I have never let anything stop me from reaching my goals. Nothing was too difficult if I just worked hard enough. But right now all I can do is second-guess myself, and to be honest, everything reminds me of Marlo. It feels like my heart has been ripped out. Yes, Leo, I have changed."

Bella grasped her hand gently, and from the look on Leo's face he was about to impart unwanted but uplifting words, yet his attention was stolen away by a small meadow smelling child popping into existence. After Ranger absently pulled her onto his knee, Anene proceeded to nonchalantly swing her feet and peruse the room, like the bored child she was pretending to be. Bella let out a clucky squeal and Leo kept firmly opening and closing his eyes as if they were broken and a sound blink would fix them. Sha casually leaned in from where he was catching up with Piper and gave his brother what he obviously thought was sound advice, "don't, call her cute, whatever you do!"

"But she is cute!" Leo replied incredulously.

That was all the rudeness Anene was willing to take, leaping from Ranger's lap, she placed hands on hips, met Leo squarely in the eye and said, "Hey burly one, are we going to have a problem here? If so, remember this, I could fuse all your toes, and then we shall see how far you can walk without balance. You will soon discover that the main function of your little toe isn't to find furniture."

Leo was speechless. Piper could be heard exclaiming, "Did she just sass the king."

Although she was enjoying seeing Leo out of his comfort zone, she made introductions, "Your highness, this is the Goddess I was just telling you about. She is fond of popping up anywhere, so unless you want a visitor in the privy, I suggest you treat her with respect."

Leo finally found his smile, bending down, he said gently, "I humbly apologise for my rudeness, goddess."

Anene adorned her I've got them right where I want them smile. Oozing delight, she purred, "You can make it up to me by giving me a kiss on the forehead and a cuddle and do not skimp on the arm pressure."

Leo carried out Anene's instructions with gusto; he was, after all, a closet hugger. The sight heralded aww sounding noises, from the occupants of the room who were unused to the little one's company. Bringing lightness and joy with her presence, Anene proceeded to do the rounds of the room, when she had everyone wrapped around her little finger, she settled at Ranger's feet, there she sat with crossed legs gently stroking a grateful Luthor. Soon after Morgan was lost to troubling thoughts, although she finally felt a semblance of safety, tomorrow she would have to rehash the worst moment of her life over and over, and this time there would be an audience.

Tomorrow came quickly, and despite a lack of sleep, Morgan found herself half awake and seated at the Protector's rightful position on Leo's right. She would have preferred to stay there, however as duty dictated she stood, and with all eyes upon her, walked into the centre room. The assembly was held in the great hall, simple enough. Not so simple was the fact that to speak you had to stand in the middle of a table, shaped like a massive ring with a gap to allow access, so you were literally, the centre of attention. There as the assembled nobility of Tornbaer watched on, she gave a full and thorough account of her mission. After adding intel about the army, she inwardly cheered herself on for successfully separating emotion from facts and patiently waited for questions. As luck would have it, Leo was the first to ask, "if you have destroyed The Master's ships, doesn't that mean that we have a lot more time to plan our next move?"

Her response ensured, no grey was in sight, "No your Majesty. The Master has other ports. The most notable is Tanye, and he has no qualms about using the people of Sirillia to get what he wants, right now that is more ships. The enemy could very well be on our doorsteps in less than a year."

Her reply sent a murmur through the room, and a few gasps escaped from the more delicate types. Engaging a typical gruffness, Hector asked, "You said that you probably destroyed the weapon used to control minds, isn't that good?"

She nodded, then responded, "Yes, that is good, but even if we have destroyed his ability to change people, he has already got most of Sirillia under his control."

The next question came from a pinched faced southern noble whom she was unfamiliar with, "Are we just supposed to believe, that what you say is true. We would not be doing our people any favours if we believed the word of one person."

The noble uttered the word one with disdain, she was used to such attitudes and her commanding response, bounced around the massive room, "You can no longer ignore the darkness on your doorsteps. The combined might of the kingdom needs to prepare for an enemy that can animate the dead, has a combined army of tens of thousands and isn't afraid to kill every one of us to get what he wants. You must act now." She would have preferred that her outburst had ended all discussion, alas it wasn't to be. The questions continued, and unfortunately they got more useless as time progressed, they discussed everything from what the Master's motivation was, to why they don't just send in assassins. By the time she made it back to her seat, she felt mentally and physically drained. Sinking into long-awaited cushioned comfort, she hoped her suffering was over. It was as she was wondering whether she had always been this impatient or was it this particular gathering that brought on such, that Morgan remembered a question to which she needed an answer. Leaning towards Hector, she whispered, "Do you want to tell me, why you are so on edge around these nobles, is it me or do you distrust them?"

After a grunt, Hector responded, "As far as I could throw them, The Guard still haven't found the person who let the acolytes into the citadel, there were quite a few delegates from nearly every duchy that day, convenient much!" She raised an eyebrow in his direction, and he continued understanding her gesture. "Yes, I know I would be able to throw some of them quite far, you know what I mean." That gave her food for thought and just before lunch too, luckily the buffet brought a full stomach and raised spirits, but then the meeting continued.

It was well into the second day of the assembly, an experience that she felt, was slowly but surely etching away her sanity. She was for the hundredth time pondering the ability of nobles to waste time when gathered in a room, time-wasting cowardly idiots the lot of them. Leo whispered in her direction bringing her out of dark thoughts, "I can see from that look upon your face, you would like to be anywhere but here, and to be honest, I would like to join you."

She smiled and replied, "We have spies in our midst and a formidable army heading our way. It is my nature to prepare. This useless posturing is torture for me. If the Lady Bonnard makes that noise that isn't her moving on her leather seat once more, I will go berserk."

Leo did well to hide his mirth in his passive gaze, but he gave it away in his whispered response, "I think she has a love for Jorn olives, but they certainly don't love her back." Disheartened he continued, "Seriously though, I thought your testimony would help, but it hasn't, we need a break to recharge, you are right this is getting us nowhere."

"The higher the climb, the more painful the fall, but boy what a view at the top." She responded pointedly. Seeing Leo's surprised look, she continued, "It was just something Marlo used to say, to give me hope."

A thoughtful expression met Leo's features. She turned her attention once again to what was happening in front of her. Not long after, she was losing a battle against heavy lids, when Leo stood up so suddenly that she jumped and grasped her staff in surprise. The room went so quiet that when Leo spoke, his voice cut through tiredness and tedium, "Enough of this, I am calling a break, time for more pleasant things, my wedding will be in two day's hence, I'm looking forward to seeing you all there." The room broke into murmurs and then the sound of a door slamming, told Morgan that Mira had left in a very hurried manner, she assumed to organise a royal wedding in less than two days. Yes, she could hear it all now, the tired murmurs of weary seamstresses, the angry cursing of the downtrodden castle staff, and of course the bellows of drill sergeants aligning their imprecise charges. Royal Wedding here we come.

. . .

USUALLY, the castle library was a place of sanctuary, Bella generally thought knowledge was one of the more impressive weapons' in her arsenal, yet today it was leaving her feeling drained and disheartened. Only now that Morgan had tasked her with finding out more information on the Master, was her quiver empty. She knew from the books which the library contained, that it was old, so much so that she regularly discovered books from the early ages, yet almost by design, there was a lack of information about certain topics. Bella was working on realigning her muddled thoughts, her chosen spot for such consisted of an alcove of cushions in the historical section of the library. She had made it hers not long after she arrived at the citadel, most avoided it, so Bella was rightly surprised when a bright orange orb flickered before her and then with a flash it was gone. She sat blinking for a moment before it reappeared a few meters in front of her. This time the orb was between a set of shelves. An unseen connection tied Bella to the object, she felt pulled to follow, and so she did. It wasn't long before the glowing ball led her deeper into what she suspected was the oldest part of the library. Abruptly as it reached a massive row of marble shelves, it disappeared, suddenly unsure she stepped up to the shelves and closed her eyes to think. She was amidst wondering if she was hallucinating when a warm feeling caressed her face. Her eyes snapped open and she looked upward, there it was again, casually beckoning her to climb. Far past questioning her actions, she followed the summoning. Using the shelves as a ladder she climbed until she reached the top. From on high, the library rewarded her with a new point of view, gracefully showed her age, in lines that stretched out, as far as the eye could see, like wrinkles older shelves made from stone and marble intermingled with the newer wood and metal examples. She was still admiring the view when the orb appeared beside her. It was so close she could touch it, so she did, unfortunately as soon as her fingers touched the warmth, it dissipated leaving a trail of unsettled dust, causing her to let out an involuntary and almighty sneeze. Her action sent more dust everywhere, as if by design during the proceeding sneezing fits, her hand gripped the shelf and happened upon a tiny slip of paper seemingly forgotten by time. Knowing the piece of history she held was her reason for being there, she cradled it, distinctly aware of its fragility. Ignoring complaining muscles she used one hand to climb back down slowly and went back to the seclusion of her pillowed alcove. Once there she opened up her hand, to find a strangely worded paragraph which looked almost as if it was, ripped from a journal of some kind.

SOMETHING STRANGE HAPPENED to me last night. Our Goddess appeared to me in a dream. She said to me, "I am sorry my child, I cannot come to you in person. Wanorde has shown himself a deceiver, his goal is control of all of Mierma, because of his actions I am unable to help directly. Do not despair if you remember us in your prayers there will always be hope." The dream was strange, to say the least, more worrying still is that a Children of Light emissary, told us that, their city has fallen and Anene has disappeared, they are in despair. If our gods have left us, we are all truly alone for what or who else can stand against a god.

THE REST of the words were stolen by time. Bella relaxed back into her cushions, mulling over the myriad of questions competing for her attention. Although she felt a need to be disheartened by the lack of substance on the paper, one word stuck out "Wanorde" she wasn't sure what the globe was trying to say. Still, she was sure about one thing; she had seen that name before.

It was some later that she awoke to comfort and move-ment. Leo's affectionate gaze greeted her when her eyes came into focus. He smiled and said matter-of-factly, "You fell asleep in the library, again." The thoughts colliding into her head must have caused a bewildered look upon her face because he continued hesitantly, "it's nothing untoward. I was just taking you to your bed."

It was then that her memory started to work, causing her to do something she never did, swear. Concerned Leo stopped walking and still unaware of her thoughts, he said earnestly, "Honest to Amare Bella, I might have given you a small peck on the cheek when I put you to bed, but you know, I am a gentleman."

"The Master is a god." She blurted out in alarm.

The bewilderment on Leo's face, caused words to continue to tumble out of her mouth, in a sudden desire to affirm sanity, "I was searching for more information on our enemy, and a glowing orb showed me to a piece of paper with the name Wanorde on it. The only reference I can find of him in this whole library is in this book of old stuff. Wanorde's followers used to call him Master. He was the only god who mistreated his worshipers. Leo, he is our enemy, I know it." Remembering to take a breath she stopped babbling long enough for Leo to take the copy of 'A complete guide to rhytiphobia and old stuff'.

Gently placing the book on the nearest shelf, Leo said, "Bell, I believe you, but I just told a whole room that we are getting married in two days and I'll be damned if I'm about to let anyone, get in the way of our happiness-."

Unfortunately for him, she had managed to find more air, cutting Leo off with her endless rant, "I know I sound crazy,

Leo, but you have got to believe-." Finally, Leo's words got through her muddled senses, and she stared at him in bewilderment, mouthing the words, "Two days." Although Leo was a gentleman, he was also an opportunist, and he took the opportunity to kiss her soundly and long. When they finally surfaced, breathlessly she chastised, "Let me down quick, I have got to report to Morgan not to mention, help your poor mother organise our wedding." Leaving Leo and his huge grin in the library, she hitched up as many layers of her skirt as she could gather and went as fast as propriety allowed. Suddenly giddy from the imagined task ahead of her, she reminded herself that none of it mattered because Leo loved her. Typically, the stepmother in her head called her out for thinking so highly of herself. This time however, excitement drowned out the lurker that was doubt. As she raced around a corner, she nearly barrelled into a very stoical looking Bob, who looked like he had another fight with Gary, nonetheless she continued past calling out in greeting. Bob watched on, amused by the sight of her barrelling down the hallway letting out the odd giggle, seemingly bereft of her senses.

YOU CAN TAKE THE GIRL OUT OF THE PIRATE SHIP

Unsettling as it was, Morgan had known it to be true as soon as Bella had uttered the words, the enemy was an honest to god, god. In hindsight, there were so many signs, the most obvious of which was something Anene had said. Cuteness be damned, she would pay more attention to the little goddess from now onwards. It was the night before the big day, and Morgan's entire crew had descended upon the Horney Sailor for pre-wedding celebrations. Typically, Denza had outdone himself, every room on the sailor's ground level was decked out with games and her already raucous crew. Primarily because her head was spinning she had taken it upon herself to escape to a side room. The main cause of said spin, was the potent effects of a cocktail Denza had designed for the occasion. He called his cocktail the spinning dick, funnily enough the room did spin therefore you felt like a dick after drinking a few. She was pulled from unusually depressing thoughts by Denza's beaming arrival. Naturally, Denza was happy to pick up a conversation, from a few hours earlier, "You are right Morgan I often think of G, even more so on the day he died."

Denza did not speak of his lost love often, and the distant look in his eye inferred he was fondly remembering, so she gently quizzed, "Do you think, there will there ever be a time when you will be able to move on?"

Sidling up next to her, Denza smiled and said in jest, "I'm not a fan of this version of tipsy Morgan, to answer your question, I'm doing ok, plus I light a candle for him every year."

Surprised she wagged a finger in his direction and slurred, "You don't strike me as the church-going kind. I remember the words I would rather visit the horn of the south than enter a church coming out of your mouth, and you hate the cold, explain yourself, sir."

A devious smile met Denza's features, and he answered, "Not church no, I have been spending a lot of time wearing a habit lately."

Suddenly understanding, she responded amidst a giggle that threatened to silence her, "Ok, when I asked you to look for Nia, I didn't think you would dress up as a nun."

Denza rolled his eyes while pursuing his lips, before feigning a lecture, "Oh please, you knew I liked to dress up, when you gave me that job, besides we both know by now we won't see Nia again."

Feeling downcast, she emitted an audible sigh and mumbled as she rested her chin on her arms, "I could do with her right about now, does everybody have to leave me?"

Having none of it Denza's fake lecture became a reality, "Woah there girl, remind me not to give you this particular mix of alcohol again. Did you ever stop to think that it was Amare you were talking to all along, and she certainly hasn't gone anywhere," Denza's features and tone softened, "Look I'm here for you, give it to me now so you can get this out of your system, what is going on in that head of yours?"

Surprising herself, she responded drawing upon the

rawness hidden beneath, "Everyone keeps saying that they have faith in me, they assume it will all be fine, Morgan will fix it. The enemy took something from me that I can't get back. I feel like that scared little girl again." Gaining momentum, she slammed her tankard down stood and vehemently continued, "When I am not afraid, I'm so damn angry that I'm scared of what I might do. You know what scares me the most, my crew will damn well follow me no matter what."

Shaking and suddenly aware, she lost all ferocity and collapsed back into her seat, a look of concern on Denza's face only made her feel worse.

Denza spoke gentle encouragement, "Do not give in to despair, when someone that close to you dies, it's so easy. The best advice I could give you right now is to keep talking and stop assuming this problem will simply fix itself. Day by day step by step you will get through this."

"I'm sorry," She said, nodding dumbly.

In true Denza style, he tried to lighten the mood, "Now that you have got that out of your system, it's time to help Bella celebrate one of life magical forces, love. Besides it's your turn, on the pole."

Rolling her eyes, she fought the inevitable, "Do I have to, you know I hate excessive drinking, not to mention those games don't mix with my competitive side."

Grabbing her hand, he yanked her from the seat and after assessing she could walk all but pushed her towards a room with a very peculiar set up. Holy Pole was an obstacle course of sorts. Crewtowners were known for holding their alcohol, and they liked to invent ways to prove such. Truth be told whoever invented it had a very sick sense of humour, luckily It would be an understatement to say that she had a competitive streak. Limbering up her muscles, she stared on determinedly visualizing the result in her mind, Yes, this she could do. Indicating the start of her round by swiftly downing two shots, a crew member counted on as she deftly positioned herself with one hand grasping the pole as high as her reach. In one sharp movement, she put all of her weight on said hand and pushed to execute the required six spins. With the room already whirling, she let go of the pole and put all her efforts into the next two shots. Walking sideways but still determined nonetheless, she continued to the second obstacle. Muscle memory took over, and before she knew it, she had managed to throw six daggers perfectly into the centre of the target. Ignoring the myriad of senses telling the contents of her stomach to vacate, she quickly downed the last shots and put all of her disposable energy into racing at a padded crew member. Executing a leap she brought both legs up to impact upon his chest, causing his momentum to push him over the line, blissfully indicating the end of her time. Placing hands on her thighs, she rested for a moment, happy that despite the fact she was about to heave she had a time even Bella would find it hard to beat. Suddenly horrified at her competitiveness, she executed a mad dash to find a bucket, the action greatly helping the queasiness in her stomach.

CHEST AND HEAD resting on the table he sighed in contentment. Ah yes, there was simply nothing better than indulging in a round of massages after using the castle baths. It was nice to get pampered once in a while, especially in the company of friends. After all the timewasting Leo had partaken in lately, this was a waste of time he could support. In stark contrast to Hector who sat quietly beside him, Aiden and Sha walked in conversing freely in the way their unlikely friendship enabled. The attendant who was dutifully seeing to Hector's needs proceeded to strike His back with a thick strap. Hector grabbed the strap firmly and with an impressive bicep on display growled menacingly, "if you whack me with that again, I will whack your face."

Secretly laughing inside, Leo put half-hearted sternness into his voice, "Hec don't, intimidate the attendants, besides that is done to encourage circulation." Hector simply gave the attendant his characteristic brooding look, the effect of which was them slowly backing away.

Always oblivious to Hector's moods, Sha chose that moment to say light-heartedly, "Seriously Hector, how do you get, your biceps so defined you have at least another third on me?"

Amused, he answered for his friend, "Hector's mother was from strong southern stock." Realizing he was touching on a sore topic, he quickly resumed, "Besides, he doesn't have a wife and has to keep up appearances, unlike you." Sha looked down at himself, then realizing that he had fallen for the ruse laughed along with the room. A while later amidst blissful quiet and calm, Aiden spoke through a drawn-out yawn, "This is nice, but what do you have in store for us next?"

Animated by the question he sat upright and responded while adjusting his towel, "I have some seriously big plans tonight lads. After this, we are going to do something I have wanted to do since my father banned me from this particular famous room of the citadel." All eyes were on him, pleased that he had piqued their interest he continued, "We are going to, raid the castle cellars." A round of blank stares, pushed him to elaborate further, "We are talking the best alcohol from every country, at every age from the cheapest swill to the most expensive tipple, this is seriously going to be epic." Looking up to see the expected excitement on their faces. Seeing only indifference, he continued all the while attempting to build suspense, "There is more after we select the alcohol of our choice, we are heading to the banquet hall. Every duchy has supplied us with their best dishes." After forgetting to breathe, he waited for enough air then continued, "Not to mention, I have organized the best entertainment I could find at a moment's notice."

His plans should have brought excitement to the room. Instead, he was disheartened by Sha's incredulous statement, "How are we brothers?"

He knew that Sha was joking, so he smiled and replied in kind, "Because, you pissed off our father so much he gave up and let you run amuck, while I had to do all the boring grown-up stuff," Sha's only response was to smirk, "Come on Sha, surely the warm puddings from Huenholm are to your liking?" Seeing a disproving scowl from Hector's direction, he added, "Don't worry, the taster has tried it all. It did give him horrible indigestion, but you can't die from that." Hector only acknowledgement was a grunt and a stretch which he was secure enough in his manhood to admit, looked pretty impressive.

Thankfully, Aiden asked the question that was on all of their minds, "Sha, what would the girls be doing right now?"

Beaming, Sha replied "I heard, last time they spent all night drinking, singing, dancing so loudly that Morgan's ears rang for days. Oh, and there is some pretty fun sounding drinking game's, especially the one with the pole," As with the others in the room, Leo's interest was piqued when the word pole was uttered.

Aiden wondered out loud, "Do you think we like them because they bring excitement to our lives."

Without hesitation, he replied, "No, I fell for Bella, the first moment, I laid eyes on her."

All murmured in agreement, Sha placed a hand on Aiden's shoulder and said brazenly, "Aiden my friend, I love Meena like a sister which is why I got to say, are you sure you want to saddle that horse again, it will continue to buck you."

Interjecting before Aiden could reply, he said, "isn't that part of the fun."

While they were all laughing at Aiden's expense, Hector abruptly stood uncaring at the fact his towel dropped to the ground, "Enough of this soppiness, sorry Leo but I'm going to the girl's party." He said brashly.

Everyone moved at once, and before he knew it he was standing before Hector's naked chest, "Where do you think you are going, it's unsafe for you to be walking the streets, right now." Hector growled.

Maintaining eye contact, as it was safer than looking at Hector's unashamed nakedness, he left no room for move-ment, "Well my friend, you oversee my security right now, do something about it."

Readjusting his towel, he cringed as Hector strode naked into the hallway and barked at the nearest guard, "I want three squads ready to go as soon as we are dressed."

The guard might have been able to keep his composure, that was until Sha called out, "And can you get someone to bring all the food, especially the pudding to the Horney Sailor." With a smile upon his face, he laughed along with his friends as they hurried to dress.

Morgan had just broken up a brawl, and with a still spinning head, she had retired from any further action to the more sedate but loud main taproom. Using the bar as a leaning post she sat beside her intoxicated friends lost in thought, Denza pulled her from pondering with a pointed comment, "You are not still sad because Bella beat you?"

As she mumbled a comment under her breath about uncanny acrobatic skills, Meena quietly giggled on the chair beside her. "I miss my children, even Darwain's smelly bum." she stated emphatically.

In response, Bella suddenly and randomly slurred, "No more floccinaucinihilipilification."

Of course, Bell's outburst pulled louder giggles from Meena, "Bell, compared to most of us, you are well-read." She reminded.

Looking apologetic Bella explained, "Sorry, I just mean I'm going to be more positive; the gods chose me to carry a weapon of legend for goodness sake." To her credit, Meena seemed to be trying to stop the chuckles, but instead, they were escaping in random, uncontrollable bursts.

Again, feeling the sadness which had hounded her all night, she sighed audibly and said, "What would Marlo be doing, about now?"

Her comment caused sombreness to descend, having none of it Denza slammed his hand down upon the bar, causing her to jump. What he did next confused her at first, but she quickly recognized the drone of Marlo's favourite bawdy song. His uncharacteristically deep voice cut through the room causing all talk to stop and ears to listen.

OH, she waits for me at Crewtown
   A little lass I know

GRINNING she summoned a voice as low and manly as she could muster and along with Bella and Meena joined in on the tune.

OH, she waits for me at Crewtown
   With her jugs on show

. . .

AT THE END of the fourth line, her crew got the idea and the tavern rung loud with the ever-increasing tempo of the song. She felt so near to Marlo at that moment. She envisaged he would be singing along in a typical slurring gruffness.

OH, I have emm in all harbours
   But my lass at Crewtown
   She lets me dock
   In all her ports

SHE WAS ABOUT to start the chorus again when the room went deathly quiet. Strolling in was the imposing form of Hector, closely followed by Sha, Leo, and finally Aiden. Momentarily two worlds collided, Leo's retinue stood in perfumed smelling finery, stark in contrast to a tavern full of tan britches and loose blouses, ominously soldiers piled in behind them. The newcomers did not come bearing weapons instead they brought all manner of fine foods. All was silent until Sha's voice cut through the awkwardness, unashamedly he sang from where they had all left off, at first his voice was the only one to ring out, then blissfully the whole room joined in, and the spell was broken.

OH, she waits for me in Crewtown.
   A little lass I know
   Oh, she waits for me at Crewtown
   With her jugs on show

THE PLACE LIT up with noise and laughter, Leo surprised her crew by brazenly walking up to Bella, and after offering his arm, he led her in a jig, they seemed ever to encircle each other as nothing else mattered. She didn't get to enjoy the sight of Bella and Leo dancing for long, because Sha walked up and flung her over his shoulder, stopping now and then to smack her bum he dropped her in the middle of the room, where she proceeded to berate him for her queasy stomach. Her lecture was silenced however when she saw Aiden walk purposely towards Meena, offering his hand he waited bravely for her reaction. Without a giggle in sight, Meena accepted Aiden's hand. Hector grabbed Taymah from the crowd and the dancing began in earnest. Shrugging she gave in to merriment and enjoyed the closeness of her husband, "Why have you got scratches on your head, and why does Meena look like she has had a bloody nose?" Sha whispered into her ear.

Smiling she replied, "You can take the girl from the pirate ship, but you can't take the pirate ship from the girl."

Deciding it best to rest her endlessly spinning head upon his shoulder, she was led around the taproom floor. The sounds of her crew's laughter carried into the uplifting night. She whispered to herself, "Wherever you are Marlo, I miss you dearly."

I AM WHAT YOU SAY I AM

The sunrise was designed to herald a perfect wedding. It was a sun shining, birds serenading, fresh bread smelling kind of morning, unfortunately for Morgan, all those things made her feel like death warmed up. Hit by waves of nausea, her hand migrated to a head under attack from millions of tiny knives, tasting a staleness also not unlike death in her mouth, she muttered, "why, why, why and what did we smoke last night?"

The concerned features of Piper came into focus before her. Unfortunately, the little princess spoke, which instantly grated her hungover and sensitive nerves, "Denza told me to give you this, as soon as you woke."

She enthusiastically accepted the special concoction that Denza aptly called night after juice, in awareness of its foul taste and odour she ensured it didn't touch the sides of her mouth, Thank you, Jaiera." She said in appreciation.

The unamused look she got back from Piper caused her to continue in a grumpy manner, "Hey, you have to get used to being called Jaiera, in Bastien at least."

"Woah, you are grumpy when you haven't had your

morning coffee, luckily Denza also gave me this," Piper replied in amusement. Producing a coffee, Piper bowed mischievously and passed it into her eager hands.

Feeling like the morning was looking up she smiled to herself and took grateful sips, then Denza's shrill voice assaulted her raw senses from the hallway, "Morgan, get your arse out of bed, you are next for hair and makeup." Piper rolled her eyes then in her usual carefree style bounced out of the room. Following Denza's panicked instructions, she tried to vacate the bed. Her every movement, followed by a groan and as her feet hit the ground, the addition of swaying caused her progress to lessen considerably. Nonetheless, she continued stumbling mostly sideways towards the dressing room. Once there, she was stuffed into a too-tight corset, dressed in a shimmering example of a few years income for most guild workers and subjected to many layers of paint on her face. Thankfully, to ensure her participation, she was also plied with a steady flow of coffee and chocolate. After her third cup of sustenance, she was finally on her way to meet up with her friends when her reflection stopped her short. In the mirror was a poised, polished and stunning example of a lady. Although she had no idea what kind of magic Denza had employed, with a smirk she grudgingly admitted to herself that she looked damn good. Light of step she moved into the main room, it was there that a floating angel in white stole her attention. Bella wore a simple silk dress which shone from underneath a delicate and understated layer of sheer lace. The lace in Bella's dress was covert in its rendition of her character, and you had to look closely to see the shape of armour subtly etched into its embroidered lines. A southern crest at Bella's lower back was the only indication of her upbringing, and the carefree happiness upon her face threatened to bring tears to Morgan's eyes. It was her job to get Bella to the church on time, so she blinked to belay the inevitable and uttered meaningfully, "Bell, you look stunning."

Before Bella could reply, Denza flew into the room, a hurricane in scarlet silk, like a madman he muttered to himself. Halting before Bella, Denza draped a veil over her head and with the flick of a wrist affixed it in place with a circlet of flowers. Bella jumped as Denza screeched close to her ear, "Ok, let's get this procession on the road shall we, when you are marrying the king, it is not ok to be late to one's wedding."

Because of a suddenly significant throb behind her temples, she fought to keep her hands from a forehead thick with makeup and said with a calmness she did not feel, "Denza darling, you look stunning in scarlet."

Visibly relaxing, Denza limply pivoted his hand at the wrist and said, "Oh, stop it."

"You know you are a walking cliché, right!" Meena said wryly.

Denza looked towards her, raised an eyebrow and replied, "Honey, this is tame, if you had my parents you would celebrate your gayness by dancing naked on the streets during market day." After another no-nonsense command from Denza, everyone thought it best to exit the Sailor quickly. A delight upon her senses, she stepped out, into a jovial atmosphere, complete with cheering crowds, waving children, adults and flags. Bella was liked, and despite the fact it took a moment to realise to whom the comment referred to, she even heard many shouts of "Peoples Protector" Funnily enough, she identified with the title more than any she had been given to date. Although it was overkill, Hector had assigned Bella's archers to line the streets, and she had to smile when she saw that each of the green-clad troops wore a new set of butterfly swords Leo had been generous with Bella's other love. The plan for the procession was to ride from the Lower City to the Citadel, against Hector's better judgement Bella rode side-saddle rather than be in a carriage. Bella wanted the people to be engaged in her wedding, even if they couldn't be at the church. Hector himself waited with Bella's Dapple Grey, holding out his hand, he helped her up onto the mare. Although Hector took his duty seriously, Morgan could see what had been clear to her since she had first seen Hector and Bella in the same room together, yet today his look of longing had an added edge, as if he was releasing himself from a possible future. When it was her turn to be helped, she placed her foot gently onto Hector's clasped hands and teased, "You know, it is my job to protect her, right?"

Hector's response was bristly even for him, "I offered because it will be my responsibility to keep her safe when she is queen, not that you couldn't do it, especially with your staff on hand."

Amused, she looked down at the small pendant which hung upon her necklace and said, "You don't miss a thing do you."

Grunting as if that was acceptable as a reply, Hector checked all was ready, before sending Bob and Gary to the front enabling him a solitary position at the rear. The cheerful procession began in earnest. The way to the Citadel was slow because Bastinian Royal weddings were characterised by small children waving ribbons and throwing petals before the procession. The people seemed desperate to look beyond unseen troubles and focus on the angel that was Ysabella Beaute Vanglassen, a cast aside Heiress, marrying Leonardis John Dallinger King of Tornbaer, The Craggy Isles, and Supreme Ruler of the Mountain Tribes.

. . .

MOSTLY BECAUSE HE wasn't a seasoned drinker, he was late, that fact was also visiting Ranger in the form of a throbbing headache and dry mouth. Making a mental note to get better at saying no to the perils of peer pressure, doubly so when it came to Morgan's crew. He continued onwards focusing on the task before him, he had one essential job this morning and already he had failed. After a hesitant knock upon Lash's apartment door, he was given an imperious look by the attendant who answered and then ushered him into a lavish reception room, where he was snobbishly told to await Lash's readiness. Uplifted by the knowledge that he wasn't the only one running late, he took a seat and politely asked for some water for his dry mouth. Although he was used to Anene's sudden appearances, he still wasn't used to the feeling of serenity her presence brought, "You were chosen for a reason," Anene said astutely.

Sighing, he said, "I know that Anene and I want to believe it, I do, but I feel useless, competent people surround me and what am I? I am nothing but a farm boy from nowhere."

Anene smiled, a typical knowing smile and replied vaguely, "Often it is the people who seem to have it the most together that are the most broken, these competent people also have fears and worries they have just grown better at hiding them. Ranger, you are not just my favourite because of your kind honourable and caring nature, you are the missing link." Grasping one of his fingers in her tiny little hand, she continued, her every word lifting him, "You are living breathing proof that nothing is impossible. I under-stand your fear, but at the time of greatest need, YOU WILL BE, the one to protect everyone. After all Ranger, they tried to kill you, but you cannot extinguish a fire that burns from within."

Nodding, he replied dumbly, "Now I understand what Morgan means by the way gods talk." After a giggle that reminded him of bells ringing, Anene responded, "Just repeat after me, Ranger. I am what you say I am."

Without hesitation, he repeated her words, "Yes, yes, you are." Anene said with a strange smile affixed. He could only respond with bewildered silence. "I'm in the mood to pat some baby animals." The little goddess announced, then flashing a dimpled grin she disappeared. Left alone with only his thoughts for company, he knew with certainty uttering those simple words caused something to shift within him. He didn't quite understand what it was yet, but he could no longer doubt himself because that meant doubting Anene.

MORGAN STOOD upon the dais with Meena and Piper at her side, although her dress was cut like Bella's it was the colour of the ocean on a stormy day. Across from her polished and looking as if they had come from an upper-echelon apart-ment stood Sha, Aiden and Hector. In the middle surrounding their friends and one stuffy looking priest was Bella and Leo. Looking on in witness, were rows of onlookers including her crew and nobles alike. She had a very ominous gut feeling, worse still she had no idea why, if anything it was all too perfect, except of course for the fact that Meena was an inappropriate wedding crier. The cere-mony started and continued without a hitch, and she was looking forward to being proven wrong because before she knew it, the proceedings had reached a part most Bastonian weddings didn't have. Bella and Leo were already formally married, but they had chosen to make declarations of love, an ancient tradition and a fitting tribute to their special rela-tionship. When it was Bella's turn to speak her voice was soft but loud enough for those that mattered to hear. Like a letter that could only be penned for Leo, she uttered simple but powerful words.

. . .

ONE DAY, I stopped and was still.
One day, I understood the meaning of it all.
One day, I learnt to lean and trust.
One day, I learnt to live unburdened.
Yes, my love, one day I found you.

YES, that did it. Morgan's tears escaped in earnest, helped along of course by Meena's sobbing beside her. Try as she might she could not regain composure, thankfully as Bella spoke her last word an almighty cheer went up from The Tempest crew, this of course surprised the flighty nobles who all but jumped out of their seats. It was as she was fighting the sudden need to laugh brought on by Meena and the nobles alike, that as it often did in such situations, time slowed. Morgan heard the arrow fly and instinctively tracked its trajectory. Although she had the ability to stop an arrow in certain conditions, it had already hit an unlikely target. For a split second she felt confusion, why anyone would want to hit a small covered table. Her confusion however, quickly turned into resignation as the dragon's fire ballooned towards her. With no time to do anything but close her eyes, it was as she heard the shouts of surprise that a warm glow could be felt upon her cheek. It felt strange to feel such physical warmth upon death. Opening her eyes again she was surprised to be in one piece if not a bit warm. The fire that was supposed to burn everyone to cinders was hovering before her angrily burning, contained somehow within a golden sphere. Her first thought was, "Was that me?" then realising she didn't even have her staff ready, she grew it to full size and brandished it. Taking stock of the room, two things quickly became apparent. First, the archer fired from above, Second, Ranger was on fire, we are not taking any usual kind of fire, he was burning a bright golden glow, there were lines on his face, and his eyes shone, the whole effect was rather beautiful. Lash reacted swiftly, sending the gift of a dagger into the chest of the archer above, he dropped, already dead onto some surprised nobles. It was then that Morgan noticed the strain on Ranger's features and panic set in. Stopping the fire from killing everyone in the room was quickly tiring him and he had had nowhere to release the energy, to which the orb contained. Acting, she slammed her staff downwards and screamed in her loudest captain's voice, "GET UNDER THE BARRIER." Erecting a large dome she pulled as much strength as she dared, all the while watching the strain on Ranger's face, her crew acted quickly pulling anyone that was to slow or on the verge's through the barrier and the safety it afforded. Ranger fell to one knee, and she screamed in his direction, "UP RANGER, UP." A look of understanding crossed his features and after a glance of his golden eyes, the orb flew through the domed roof above and continued on a trajectory that she knew to be seaward. Glass and rubble fell downwards onto her barrier, most of which followed the dome's curve towards the edges of the room. Spent Ranger collapsed and consequently his golden glow dissipated. Lash quickly ensured he was alive then protectively stood over him, fresh daggers produced and at the ready. Aware her shield had a limit, Morgan's crew were already working to vacate the room. Finally when all were clear and safe, she slowly decreased the size of the barrier, then after ensuring she was safe dropped it entirely. Weak and trembling, her work was not done. Reading her mind, Bella ripped the veil from her head and called out, "Morgan this way." Meena and Hector followed behind her leaving everyone else to maintain sanity and belay confusion. Bella seemed to know every short cut to the stables, once there they appropriated the handiest horses and went barrelling towards the royal docks and their destination, The Tempest.

Meena rode up beside Bella and said matter-of-factly "You are a queen, you know."

Bella replied, "What?" Meena spoke louder, this continued thus, until Meena's voice reached Bella's ears and everyone else's within earshot, despite what was happening around them, they giggled in earnest.

Reaching her ships mooring, she pulled her horse up sharply and leapt from its back. Racing up the gangplank, she turned her senses to any signs of danger, despite the fact four skeleton crew were on duty no one waited. On it continued thus, and yet no one could be found until they reached the upper hold. There where the dragon's fire was stored, they found her crew, all dead next to where a missing barrel of dragons fire should have been.

Her frustrated scream rang out into the morning. Someone would pay for this, turning to her friends she mused, "Do you remember that job we did for that dandy on Jorn?" They nodded catching on, and she continued, "Good, it seems we have a wedding reception to attend ladies, Meena can I trust you to pick up that thing from Denza's warehouse?" As Meena nodded her affirmation, Hector looked on trying to make some sense of the secret language they were all suddenly speaking. Her eyes narrowed amidst unsavoury thoughts. No one struck at her heart and came away unscathed. Yes, she had changed; it was time to accept it and show her enemy just how much.

YOU DON'T PLAY FAIR

She waited, disgusted by the sight of gentry lacking the ability to close their mouths while chewing, I mean really, she mused, even with her upbringing she had the manners to eat with her mouth closed. Just a few more bite's Morgan thought to herself. Finally, there it was, she was rewarded with a satisfying sight, all around the banquet hall, nobles were falling asleep, some into their puddings. She may have been enjoying the sight a little too much, because she was amidst disagreeing with her inner self about her distaste of the aristocracy, when Leo said pointedly, "I would love it if we could get this over with, what's the plan here?"

Nodding, she replied, "First for safety reasons its best if we check if they are all asleep, from there, I will touch them with my staff."

"Won't your staff kill them?" Leo asked concernedly.

Somewhat offended by the implications of his question, she bristled, "I will be quick just in case or were you thinking, we should strip them all right here and search for dots?" Leo looked panicked. She continued in earnest, "Look, I have to be honest, after all this, if we do have to try to change them back, some may not make it are you prepared for that outcome, I cou-"

Cutting her off with a raised hand, Leo said resigned, "This is my burden to bear Morgan, so let's get this done."

Standing up, she motioned for those waiting in strategic places to proceed. After each person was rescued from their pudding and checked for signs of sleep, she followed behind, lightly tapping them with her staff. Before long the action sent a young southern noble into fits, quickly withdrawing she indicated that he be separated, onwards it continued thus. She was only a quarter of the way through the room when Ajaib jumped up from his pretend sleep, to lunge at Taymah. Meena who was Taymah's backup, was equal to the task, blocking Ajaib's thrust, she sliced back with one of her own, the fight was on in earnest, guard and crew alike scrambled to give the fighter's room, no one wanted to get amongst the quick-paced action. She was surprised to see that the man from The Craggy Isles had considerable ability, if this was his sword skill she was glad of one thing, he had no spear. Really, who ever heard of a spear-wielding sheep herder. Before long she was tapping her foot impatiently, the bout was taking too long, every moment it continued was a moment that the sleepers in the room could wake. Meena would soon get the upper hand, but she couldn't wait, at her nod, Castain came up from behind and whacked Ajaib soundly with the pommel of his sword. The result of Castain's action was a satisfying heap on the ground. Meena gave her an unamused look but thankfully kept quiet. Walking up to said heap she tested her staff, nothing, no movement of any kind not even a facial twitch, confused she proceeded to give him another prod, still nothing. It was after her third prod, that confusion set in, "That's strange?" She declared.

Curious Leo asked, "What's strange?"

"I could have sworn he was one of the master's puppets." She replied.

Her bewildered comment sent Leo into an uncharacteristic but rather non-committal rant, "That's a bit discriminatory. What, because he wears black and always has a neutral demeanour. What's next, you want me to ban dark cloths and dead-eyed stares."

Holding up her hands, she soothed, "Woah there, I'm sorry, I wasn't trying to offend."

"No it's me that should be sorry, it's just a little disconcerting seeing your court like this," Leo replied, seemingly regaining his composure.

Glancing around at the odd scene before her understanding dawned, "You are right, let's get this finished as quickly as possible," She affirmed.

Later, the task was complete, and six nobles had been separated from the rest of the court, including the disconcerting sight of the Duke of Dulcea. It was the worst kind of news imaginable, Wanorde had managed to infiltrate to the highest level of Leo's court. She was still reeling from the news when the room started to show signs of wakefulness. Hector called for Wanorde's minions to be taken to the cells; this would have enabled Leo some time to decide their fates. Unfortunately, fate had other plans. Kritchner Bonnard awoke, worse still he found the inhuman strength required to snap his bindings. After stealing a sword from an unsuspecting guard, the Duke went barrelling straight as an arrow towards her, "The master sends his regards," He spat, with hate-filled features.

Instinct quickly overtook surprise, running to meet him, she re-joined, "One thing the master has taught me recently." Grounding her staff under momentum, she vaulted over him and completed her sentence, "When it comes to him, I don't play fair." Her action had given the occupants of the room time to bear weapons. It didn't matter, however, because the Duke only had dark resolve towards one person, Morgan. As he again bore down, instinct again engaged, splitting her staff at one end she sent the produced dagger, into the Duke's shoulder. To wound, would have matched her intent. Unfortunately, she wasn't so lucky, collapsing he writhed on the ground to the degree that even a contortionist would be impressed, the accompanying scream was so alien if the nobles weren't already awake that did the trick. Some of the gentries sat bolt upright as if waking from a nightmare. Unfortunately for them, it was more like a nightmare they woke up to. Not one to disappoint, not only did the Duke proceed almost to combust he dared to produce the most putrid smelling vapour. Eventually, the ghastly noises subsided, and all that was left of Kritchner Bonnard was a small pile of black ash and his clothes. It was no longer in doubt to the suddenly awake room, Wanorde existed, and as the end of her staff re-appropriated itself, she glanced towards Leo fully intending to apologise. Yet, the sight of every eye fixated upon her, caused words to flee.

He was engaging in his favourite pastime, hiding in the shadows listening to gossip, at first it was to get some post excitement opinions, after that, it was for his amusement. The great hall was buzzing with nobles complaining about pudding stains and Morgan having the audacity to put the room to sleep without seeking the King's permission. That particular version of events made Aiden smile, mainly because he knew Morgan enough to know it was the sort of rumour she approved off. Although Aiden was sure the festivities would go late into the night he wasn't feeling particularly festive there was nothing like seeing someone melt before your eyes to remind you of the fact, that it could have been you. Ranger was resting on a chair in the corner of the room and the sight of Lash fussing made him smile, Ranger had been allowed to join the celebrations as long as he rested and Lash had taken it upon herself to ensure that he did just that, to the point where she had commandeered a team of attendants to cater to his every simple whim. Disengaging from blending in, Aiden sidled over to Ranger and said earnestly, "I am glad you are on our side, my friend, that was some pretty impressive stuff you did back there." Typically, the farmer smiled shyly and gave his thanks. He was about to follow-up with some questions that would have helped quell curiosity when Taymah rudely interrupted in a tone that demanded answers, "Aiden, what are they waiting for, all the men are just standing there, staring at us, why don't they talk to us, or ask us to dance?"

Being from a family with ties to royalty, this was a topic he had an intimate knowledge of. He replied assertively, "That's easy they are nobleman. Their mummies emasculated them, till a fear of rejection crippled them into a state of indecision."

Although it was an improvement on giggling, he was unused to the sight of Taymah gobsmacked, when she finally found her voice she used it to berate him, "Wow, that's a wildly unpopular opinion and a gross generalisation." He felt only relief as Taymah stormed away, with her ever-present shadow in the form of Brady in tow. He was still staring at their backs when a voice caused his heart to leap.

"I see, you finally managed to despatch your groupies."

There was only one response he could give to Meena's observation, "So I have, what a pity." He was entirely unable to keep the goofy grin from his face.

Meena looked at him for a second and seemed on the verge of actually conversing with him. It was then that his ex-girlfriend who was a looker but was low in anything upstairs, rudely interjected as if Meena was invisible, "Oh Aiden my darling, I have been looking everywhere for you. I see you have only managed to get more dashing. As always, the mere sight of you is enough to cause a maid to swoon."

Not taking his eyes from Meena's, he replied absently, "Hello Prudence it's been, what a few years, why don't you go and find a nice Duke's nephew to talk to."

Not that bright, Prudence continued with more compliment vomit, "Oh you are silly darling, why would I do that when I could be in your company, I have come to ask if I could watch you train sometimes, that was my favourite thing remember?"

He daren't take his gaze from Meena, although it was against his nature, he did the only thing he could think of, employ rudeness, "Prudence, In case it isn't obvious to you, I don't subscribe to flattery anymore, go and flirt with someone who gives a damn." Thankfully, Prudence huffed and stomped away, like a spoiled child.

It was as he was breathing a sigh of relief that he let his gaze slip, it was too late to rectify his mistake by the time Meena's small but sharp fist found his ribcage. As he clutched his side in pain, Meena sauntered off with an uncharacteristic grin affixed. When understanding dawned, and he could breathe again, he joyfully exclaimed, "She likes me!"

Castain, who saw the whole interaction, helped him to a chair, "Oh boy, are you in for a ride." Castain placated, while gently patting him on the back. He could only chuckle at Castain's choice of words, then flinch from the pain his mirth brought.

So much harmony and beauty at this moment. So many whom she adored and most importantly, so much to lose if her plans failed. Morgan was perusing the celebrations before her, seemingly unable to find herself. Leo's apt words pulled her to awareness, "You seem more relaxed, which means you have formulated a plan."

In the awareness that Leo was in tune to subtle mood changes, she adopted a deliberate, thoughtful look and responded meaningfully, "Formulating as we speak."

Leo saw right through her, "I know you have limited experience with close-knit families Morgan, but you are a Dallinger now, that means we will always have your back."

Damn Leo and his uncanny understanding of the human condition, it would have been so easy just to cave right then and there, to confide in him. The fact was that even she was afraid to voice the inevitable truth of what she was feeling. Even worse, Leo stood up and did something he never did in front of mask inducing gentry; he hugged her. She felt so safe at that moment and yet Sha's comment from her opposite side, brought more warmth to the moment, "I've been trying to do that since she rescued me."

Of course, then it was Sha's turn, he had even fewer qualms about embracing in front of nobles, their adoration only firmed her resolve, leaning in she said in a hushed tone which only Leo could hear, "I can't relax Leo, not until this is finished."

Leo reply was annoyingly apt, "You forget Bella has told me much about your adventures, you always put others needs before your own, you don't have to do that anymore, you have Sha, you have me, and now you have your father." Nope, Leo was going to have to do better than that, thankfully in true Leo style he did not push, he simply left her to mull.

Alas, her moment's peace was fleeting, Sha leaned in and said, "Soooooo, we need to talk."

Smiling at how uncomfortable Sha was, at trying to

initiate a serious conversation, she replied using humour to deflect his intent, "No, you can't get a cannon for our parlour."

Sha usually enjoyed such banter, but there was concern laced in his reply, "Ah no, that wasn't what I wanted to talk about, that is however, a bit of a let-down, I wanted to see how you are doing, it feels like you have been hiding from me lately."

She was getting a little worn by maintaining a façade, and this was Sha, her faithful rock, so she found a truth she hoped he could understand. Leaning in to rest her weary head upon Sha's shoulder, she said, "The truth is, I missed you so much even after we rescued you, I was afraid to accept you were safe in case it was all somehow a falsehood, yes I am aware that sounds silly." Her admission sent him into an uncharacteristic silence, so she continued, "Otherwise I'm good, all things considered, a little tired to be honest, this staff takes it out of me, missing the little ones-."

Hitting the nail on the head, Sha interrupted her, to execute a nonsensical rant, "Yeah about those weapons, you kind of had me worried there, how does that thing work exactly, I mean that was some pretty serious stuff." She raised an eyebrow, usually an obvious signal of her annoyance, Sha missed it. Instead, he babbled onwards, in ever-increasing absurdity, "How do you know that thing isn't controlling your mind, it could be taking years of your life away, until one day poof."

Fighting to keep the amusement from her voice, she Interjected, "Aren't I acting like myself?"

"No, you are not." Sha replied abruptly.

Understanding dawned, of course, he thought she was acting strange, she was still in fight mode and had not taken stock of the otherworldly things that were happening around her. Adopting what she thought was her best calm tone she said, "I promise you, how I am acting has nothing to do with my staff, when I use it, it feels like I am simply choosing to tap into something much greater than myself. I am in control the whole time. I'm just feeling a little weary that's all, you would too If you had an army to worry about, another two generals of Wanorde's to stop."

Sha cut her off before she could add to her growing list of fears, "You mean we, right, we have those things to worry about, you can't take all that stuff solely upon your shoulders."

"I'm ok Sha, besides you know what I say if you can't see the wood for the trees chop down the forest." She replied, heartened by his concern, but feeling rather over his line of questioning.

A typical grin graced Sha's features, "Ok now I know you will be ok, that was one of the annoying analogies that you like to use when you are trying to evade a question."

She re-joined, rolling her eyes at Sha's mockery, "Seriously I'm fine, besides I have my friends, my coffee, my husband and a few gods helping out here and there, we will be ok."

Even though she accentuated the word "we", Sha's response infuriated her further, "Wait what, did you just put coffee and friends before me?"

BY YOUR LEAVE

$\mathcal{M}$organ stood before a room lacking in inappropriate mumbles and poorly hidden whispers, her actions at the banquet had left no doubt she was dedicated to eradicating an enemy that was not a figment of her imagination. She spoke before the assembled nobles ensuring all heard her astute words, "Today I thought I would speak about our enemy, but I think my display was enough to show you the reality of the situation. Instead, I have asked Lashima Shllashan, The Desert Rose to speak on what we can't see, but will be our reality if we don't act."

No one uttered a word. All eyes followed Lash as she purposefully strode through the gap and into the centre of the room. The princess was trained in public speaking. Lash commanded the assembly's attention her every word appealed to their humanity and was backed up with facts that could not be disputed, "Only one word sums up the reign that would be Wanorde's if you allowed him here. Death, we are dying in unimaginable numbers, our crops are wilting, our land is drying, water is seemingly disappearing from even the most plentiful sources. My people are killed for nearly every reason but mostly because humans are hated. My people are quite simply being wiped from this earth. The Master's every breath is hell-bent on our destruction. You might ask why don't we just bow down now and let him win. I have an understanding of that as well, to be under his control is to know with certainty the moment he has total dominion overall, you become useless and death would find you soon after."

Shortly after Lash had finished speaking the assembly voted unanimously in favour of mobilising the country into war. Despite the negative connotations of such a decision, Morgan felt a weight lift from her shoulders, another piece of her plan had fallen into place, and she was free to move onwards, into the next bold but dangerous move. Even better, she would soon see her children. The combined assembly had been swift in making decisions, including the appointment of General Freeholme. The Plains Herd were given the power to oversee the war camp which was to be erected outside of Bastien. It was a good call considering they lived in roving bands and also enabled those well versed in warfare were in charge of such. The final decision was an immediate upscale of shipbuilding. As Baron of Crewtown, Sha was given the unenviable task of employing diplomacy to mobilise the Mountain Tribes into helping him build as many ships as possible, indeed if anyone had the charisma to do such, it was Sha.

Back at the royal apartments, the room was abuzz with the news of the day. All seemed to be trying to drink in each other's company before the inevitability of leave-taking. Lash was the first to offer Morgan her goodbyes despite the fact she had only known her a short time it was sad to contemplate her departure, "I am going back home. That speech just made my decision clearer, Ranger has asked to tag along, and it seems he will be good protection,"

Catching the twinkle in Lash's eye, she replied wryly, "Yes, he will be good company as well, I'm sure." Waiting for understanding to appear upon Lash's features, she continued, "But seriously, I am going to miss you two. Please keep me updated on what is happening. Our next move depends on good intel. Take Aquila if he will go with you, he is the only bird that doesn't require ship to ship flight, and he will find me fast if you need me."

Lash's smile lit up her face, and she spoke with warmth, "Of course I can do that, thank you for making me feel like a friend, you truly are a sister of my heart."

After embracing Lash, she watched her move away, lost to her worries, Castain's knowing words guided her back to the present, "They will be ok, I have loaned them The Serpent and its handpicked crew."

"Thank you for that. We need all the friends we can get, we are all nearing hazardous waters." She said, gratefully. There was no time like the present, so she brought up a prickly subject, "so i've been thinking." Castain raised an eyebrow but thankfully stayed silent, so she continued, "If I, a humble captain's bastard, can rise to the heights of Protector of the Realm and marry a prince then why can't you similarly rise. We both know despite your distaste for nobility you are still in love with Mira, heck the whole world knows by now."

Castain's usual stoic reply was abandoned for something she was entirely unfamiliar with, fatherly advice. Gently grasping her shoulders, Castain spoke as if he could read her thoughts, "I know you are planning something dangerous, which is why you are trying to speed things along with Mira and me among other things. Morgan, I need to make sure you understand something that has been weighing on me. I have never liked the negative connotation of the word bastard. It means an illegitimate child as if somehow it's the child's fault. What I am trying to say is, to me, you were always legitimate. Look, I'm not going to demand you tell me what is going on, I know you too well, just promise me whatever your next move is you will be careful."

Struck dumb by Castain's honestly, all she could say was, "I promise, dad." There it was, a straightforward word, although it slipped out it felt so right at that moment. Falling into a comfortable silence, they shared a moment of harmony. After a while, she asked tentatively, "As I imagine Sha, is about to get very busy in negotiations with the mountain tribes, I'm going to take you up on your offer and take the children to Hautbas to see their great grandparents while they are still alive. Besides I have always wanted to go there but never seemed to find the time." She didn't voice the thought that kept repeating like an interloper in her mind, "*you mean, while you are still alive.*"

Castain cracked a rare smile and responded favourably, "Fair enough. I think after what you have been through lately you deserve some time away. Besides Sha did leave you to run Crewtown then got himself kidnapped."

Smiling, she said, "Good, we are agreed, I will go to Hautbas, you will stay here to cultivate relationships if you get my meaning."

Castain's smile widened, and he replied, "Deal, I will request that your grandmother doesn't annoy you too much, in return you can relax, you aren't even twenty-five, and you have lived so many lives, do not put so much pressure on yourself." If only he knew that truth, the pressure had lifted, in its place was only grim determination. Leaving Castain to rendezvous with Mira in the favoured window spot, Morgan joined up with Meena and Bella, sadly an understanding of the fact they would soon be leaving each other overshadowed their banter.

That was until Anene appeared before them and announced, "I thought it best to give my goodbyes while they are going around. I have already stayed too long, Hanan is angry with me, it is so bothersome, not to mention Amare will have that disappointed look on her face, she is holier than thou." Anene looked up at her, she suddenly felt silly standing over the little goddess and knelt to huggable level. The embrace she received was warmth incarnate, she was sure it was not possible to feel so safe, that was until the little goddess used the opportunity to whisper into her ear, "You can trust us, Morgan."

Nodding dumbly, she replied, "How can I place my faith in you, there are so many situations when I felt powerless, what if Ranger collapsed before I put the barrier up, or I ran out of energy."

Anene's poignant reply slid under her guard, "Silly Morgan, energy is not a concept a god is aware of, ponder that. You think by running away, you are protecting every-one. Still, the truth is no matter what happens, for better or worse, it was always your destiny. Need I remind you Amare foresaw your every decision, your every fall and most impor-tantly your every triumph. I won't be seeing you for a while but remember from all of us we will always be here for you."

Tears threatened, she suddenly found herself in a battle to maintain composure amidst a room full of people she was already hiding from. Finally released from the hug she held Anene at arm's reach and said pointedly, "Why don't all you gods, Just fix this now, before there is more death."

Anene's reply was mercilessly simple, "Do not mistake, a god's exact timing for things." After emphasising her point by tapping a small finger upon the tip of her tiny nose, she turned and walked purposely up to Bella. Placing her hands upon her hips, the little goddess said, "Your stepmother's voice, is a symptom of your feelings of undeserving, soon like a child of light, you will shine much brighter than any mere queen is able." At first, Bella's only response was a shy smile, then she paid the price for the little goddess's wisdom, one embrace with no skimping on the arm pressure.

After their turns were up, the three friends watched as Anene made her rounds on her mission to impart her gems upon the other occupants, "Anene thinks because she's adorable she doesn't have to hold back on the punches," She said matter-of-factly.

Bella replied absently, "Do you think, we will ever see her again?"

"Yes, I'm sure we will." She replied, more hopeful than sure.

Meena giggled, when her friends looked in her direction she explained, "I just got a mental image of what she'll be doing when we meet her next, patting baby animals of course."

It was as their giggles were dying down that Anene finished exacting her fee from the occupants of the room, after a mock bow in Leo's direction the goddess said in fake pomposity, "By your leave, your highness," Then with a flash of dimples, she was gone.

"She clearly knows, what that means," Leo said wryly, although the room laughed along with him, she was sobered by the knowledge that when she saw Anene again, it would be in darker times.

Strolling over to Sha, Morgan interlocked an arm and said, "I think we should head home to our fiefdom and our children."

With a smile that told her, he was up to no good, Sha replied, "That's if we still have a home."

The confusion must have been evident upon her face because Sha explained himself, "Don't tell me you didn't wonder if Arlo has taken control of Crewtown in our absence."

In mock jest, she turned and called out to the nearest

runner, "Run and find my first officer, the Tempest lifts away in an hour." The widening grin upon Sha's features brought a roll to her eyes.

MORGAN'S first sight of the familiar scape caused a grateful breath, these mountains symbolised home safety and security, even if they were looking sparse and ruined by the change that winter had brought. As she watched Crewtown come into focus she mused that it seemed unfair that the trees were stripped naked by a thief called autumn, then after such carelessness, their leaves were left to rot, if that wasn't bad enough, an interloper called winter brought a bone-chilling blanket of white. Downhearted she pulled the strings of her jacket tighter and longed for the uplifting things that spring would bring including, warm skinned heat and newness in the form of baby animals. As always, an inner voice reminded her that there were trials on the horizon and she could not sit idly by when planning was afoot. To that effect as soon as her foot hit the platform, she had thrown herself into formulating plans. Unfortunately for her, one of her first agonising tasks happened to be a remembrance service to honour those who had died, despite immeasurable efforts she could not shake the feeling that she was failing Marlo, mostly because there was absolutely nothing that could be planned that measured up to the lives he saved. In the end, she stood with the rest, as the flaming rum-soaked pyre's moved out into the harbour, their sombre glow matching a chilly winters day and when all was observed the service itself was completed with undeniable Marlo flare. Every single cannon fired a volley into the night was loaded with Marlo's concoction of a powder for testing and special occasions. In that deafeningly bright moment, overwhelming gloom turned into uplifting daylight.

Not long afterwards, the funeral-goers retired to the only place that seemed appropriate, the Rose & Tickle. It was expected of her to give the first speech. Yet, when Morgan stood, she was struck dumb by emotion. It was all too real. Bracing herself she pulled strength from a desire to do Marlo proud, thankfully the clock in her mind ticked again, and she spoke in raw and miserable honesty "Marlo Oryn, you would do this to me of all people." Too early the tears threatened, she commanded them to retreat and continued, "Your pet names for us were always birds we were your sparrow, your pelican, or your skylark, better yet we were and always will be your family. I need to say my friend that I will always look for you, I will look for you in the shape of the clouds, I will look for you to ignore a command or disagree with me when I'm facetious, I will look for you when I feel a vibration through the ship that you would want to tweak." Murmurs from the occupants of the room signalled their agreeance. She continued in defiance to her tears, "I will look for your unbiased opinion and the sheer lack of filter upon your mouth. Most of all, I will look for you to guide me like you have done ever since we started our adventures. Marlo, you were my first and an excellent example of a father, and for that I will always be grateful. You used to say Hanan's rest gives you freedom from stupidity, well I hope you are free, father of my heart." Raising her glass high, she said, "To Marlo" The room echoed her words and all drank to their departed friends. Sitting back to nurse her drink she was quickly lost in her thoughts, those that spoke were unheard, no one could bring her outwards, until Sha said gently, "The Family Vault, you know the one we use for storage and the like."

Confused by Sha's comment, she asked, "What?"

Sha continued, his words warming her, "I have requested it be turned into a burial vault, I know it's empty, but I asked them to start by adding a spot for Marlo, so you have some-where to go when you need to remember him, that is until the statue is finished. Of course, the statue will be put up outside the Rose." Nodding dumbly, she rested her head on his shoulder, sighed and thought on the fact that it was going to be a long year, hell it was going to be a long winter.

IF AIDEN WAS honest with himself, he was tipsy, these Crewtowner's knew how to commiserate, and if he were even more honest, he would have to admit for once in his life he had followed a woman. He should have been working from his cushy office extracting information for the upcoming war. However, according to the letter he had just received, he was doing his job by merely being in Crewtown, go figure. He was about to call it a night and was contemplating how to make it to his room without a constant supply of walls for leaning when he saw her standing beside him. Meena's arms were crossed, and she was eyeing up his favourite dagger. To sway less, he used the bar to lean on and said with as much articulation as he could muster, "oh, you like that dagger do you, then you should come to see the ones in my room at the castle." It took him a moment to understand the need for mirth from those around him, to rescue propriety, he exclaimed, "I mean, feel free to take what you need." Oh, boy, was he digging himself a hole but he wasn't going to quit now, so he rightly continued to fire out more words in the vain hope the right mix saved him from embarrassment, "I mean, you can throw money at me if you like."

The laughter had reached a heady level, and wonders never cease Meena came to his rescue. Placing herself under his arm, she guided him towards the door, "Aiden, I think we need to talk about etiquette," She said casually.

Offended, he slurred, "I can assure you, I do good etiquette."

Meena continued to guide him onwards and replied, "Yes but not pirate or sailor etiquette, it's a good rule to think more than twice before you say things, and in your case, think again before you speak." Her helpful advice was uplifting, to say the least, conjoined with the fact she was helping him get to bed. The joy he felt was almost enough to drown out the laughter that followed them.

MORGAN HAD BEEN a gracious host she had even appropriated a large building on the academy campus for him and his charges. In return, he had made himself useful quickly busying himself with a role as an instructor and even found the need to make Dragons Fire again, all in all, Tenanu was happy with his new life. The children themselves quickly became essential to the day to day running of the academy doing everything from running errands to setting up the classes they showed themselves ever the hard workers, Tenanu knew them to be. He saw greatness in their futures, yet often a glance at one of the parentless in his care was all it took for him to remember the darkness that he saw on the horizon.

THE END

GLOSSARY

PEOPLE

MORGAN JONES – Captain of The Tempest a merchant ship, AKA Bloody Mary Captain of The Brothel Beauty a pirate ship used for nefarious purposes. AKA Albatross. Protector of the Realm, Baroness of Crewtown.
RENA SLATER – proprietor of the Rose & Tickle in Crewtown.
MEENA FARSEED – AKA Sparrow Morgan's best friend Meena was brought up as a black cloak trained as soon as she could hold a sword, she uses two identical swords adorned with ribbons that she uses with a distinct fighting style called Yuiani which looks like dancing only deadlier.
BRIA – Rena's pet Barmaid
MARLO ORYN – Second in command of The Brothel Beauty/ The Tempest, commonly referred to as Morgan's second afraid of heights, yet he is a half breed man giant that towers above most. Inventor of the combustion chamber or fire chamber that powers the new flying ships, and various other inventions.

BELLA – AKA Ysabella Beaute Vanglassen/Skylark, originally brothel girl, friend of Morgan Jones, bastard child of a noble taught archery by her father from a young age until she was cast out by her stepmother when he died. Commander of an elite group of archers based in Bastien.

ASHARN ROBERT DALLINGER – Baron of Crewtown and Prince of Tornbaer first in the line to the throne, AKA Sha.

LEONARDIS JOHN DALLINGER – King of Tornbaer and The Craggy Isles and Supreme Ruler of the Mountain Tribes, known for his gentle but fair nature and intellect, loves hunting although that runs in the family.

HERNE JAMISON DALLINGER – King His Royal Highness died in the hour of blood. Father to Leo Sha and Jaiera and husband to Mira.

FIFE JORN DALLINGER - Duke of Rollston, a duchy in Tornbaer Killed in the hour of blood, aligned himself with the evil known as the Master, little is known about why or how.

JAIERA MAYBLE DALLINGER – Princess of Tornbaer AKA Piper Jones, raised by Morgan Jones.

RORG – The deceased previous owner of The Tempest/Brothel Beauty he was a highly feared captain.

SAILORS or CREW – Gruth and Aroon from Rorgs Original Crew, Brady, Ameile, Cheese, Sam, Laiken, Taymah.

MIRA ROSE DALLINGER – Leo's Mother – Trained by the Sisterhood of Amare. Born in Dulcea Northern Tornbaer originally Mira Rose Bonnard.

DENZA ANNIAS – Proprietor of the Horney Sailor, a tavern near the docks of Bastien also a black-market bootleg operator and proprietor of secrets.

LUTHOR – Leo's prized hunting dog.

AIDEN MAYNAEIR – Noble and Spy Master to the King of Tornbaer.

ARLO – Nanny to Morgan and Sha's triplets. Aiden's ex manservant.

AQUILA – Eagle from Hanan a group of almost impassable mountains behind Crewtown. Hanan eagles are very rare and pure white. Aquila is special as he can speak and is very opinionated when he does.

HERMES – Leo's Prized Hunting Horse from Plains Herder stock, Specially trained as a Chieftains Horse.

GARY and BOB - Guards at the Citadel, both used to be porters in the king's army they have seen much action in Sirillia.

REGINALD JAMES CUISINIER THE THIRD – Lord of Hautbas famous swordsman it was said none was his equal, His family's estates are in Hautbas in the Dulcea region of Tornbaer. AKA Castain, Captain of The Serpent

COMMANDER ORTON – Commander of the Garrison at Astrom under the sway of the master.

AREW – Merchant of Hard to acquire goods at Astrom also an obsolete word for Arrow.

LASHIMA SHLLASHAN - Princess of the Storm, Princess of the Reshda Desert Tribe and The Desert Rose AKA Lash

KING JAEGAR HENRY DALLINGER – King Herne's Father, died in a hunting accident.

HECTOR JAMES DALLINGER - Bastard son of Fife Dallinger the previous treasonous Duke of Rollston and new duke, friend to Leo.

THE MASTER – This guy is pretty darn evil; besides the fact he can bend your mind to his nefarious purposes and is in control of most of Sirillia not much else is known about him.

DARRAN AND RANDALL – commanders of the Tornbaern Archers. Both exceptional with the bow and despite their humble beginnings born to lead.

TALLULAH – The hunting dog given to Bella by Leo, she is one of Luthor's brood.

GARETH FAREYA and DARWAIN – Sha and Morgan's Triplets watch out.

TANNER YADRO – Marlo's brilliant apprentice according to Marlo a little too brilliant.

RANGER – Farm boy from Jerone on the edge of the Leviraan Desert in Sirillia likes his simple life and a village girl.

THE FOUR – Common term for the four Kings and Head of the Master's Loyalists.

KURJA FARSEED – One of the Four. Self-appointed King of the Black Cloaks, Meena's estranged father, Killed in combat.

BLACK CLOACKS – Loyal solders of the Master.

AIDAS – One of the four Kings of the Master, Head of the dark Acolytes.

DARK ACOLYTES – Dark Casters of the Master's army.

ANENE – Goddess commonly known for Happiness, relationships and ardour, she likes baby animals, hugs and kisses and popping in unannounced.

AMARE – Goddess commonly known for Healing, love and Dreams. Not much is known about Amare she like to make an appearance only when there is great need.

SHEV – Old retired sailor owner of a fleet of boats, very bored in his retirement.

LEOLA JONES – Mercenary and Morgan's mother not much is known about her short of her poor treatment of Morgan as a child.'

HANAN – God mostly in charge of afterlife although not much is known about Hanan his sibling's mention on occasion that he has a temper and tends towards action rather than words.

TENANU – an elderly prophet and dragons fire brewer, his tribe hails from the Judian Desert.

LADY MARGARETE VANGLASSEN – Baroness of the dutchy of Aanlyis, Bella's overbearing stepmother.

Kritchner Debou Bonnard – Duke of Dulcea/Northern Kingdom – resides over Dulcea from the Gatehouse.
AJAIB SARESTRA – Master of the Sword of the Gatehouse – Hailing from the Craggy Isles
GUIJUI FREEHOLME - the Chief of the plains heard, even though there are many chiefs all the chiefs who want to be top dog, get together and fight it out, to most it's an excuse to drink a lot.
G – or Garth was the love of Denza's life a story for another time or book.

PLACES

MIERMA – The world which this story is set, it has two moons various Deity's, Gods and Goddesses, although most are related.
TORNBAER - A large Continent of which the capital city is Bastien, Tornbaer is strong in commerce engineering or magic depends who you ask. Tornbaer is currently ruled by the Dallinger family, it has many secrets most include random landmarks of which no one has any idea how they got there, such as the North and South Bridges in Bastien.
CREWTOWN – Kingdom city which is quickly growing. Home to and ruled by Morgan and Sha Dallinger as well as fisherman and a growing community of would be swinging sailors or Flighties the term given to those who crew the growing population of flying and non-flying Kingdom Ships that are built in the Crewtown Shipyards, they all share in a synergetic relationship of sorts. A relatively secure port primarily because of the impossibility to get a large force through the Gap without incurring heavy casualties. Crewtown has only one entrance/exit the sea.
THE GAP - Entry to Crewtown from the sea, there are cliffs

on both sides at the seaward entry onto the gap the cliff walls almost touch at the top.

BASTIEN – The capital city of Tornbaer, broken into The Upper City, The Lower City and The Citadel the most notifiable landmarks are two bridges which ships sail under, the Canals which connect most of the lower city and the Citadel which sits atop a rocky crag jutting out seaward.

THE CITADEL – A large castle in Bastien seat of the Dallinger family, the citadel is broken into four parts The Guest Quarters, The Royal Apartments which faces the sea at the back of the castle, The Servant's Quarters, and The Common Quarters where you enter the castle and the throne rooms is. The Long Hall connects all of these and is made up of two long halls connecting in the middle.

THE GATEHOUSE – A Large Castle in Dulcea twice the size as the Citadel complete with a racing track on one side as well as lake and lots of grandiose gates.

Huenholm – The seat of power in the South, basically a high wall against a mountain the castle itself is carved out of the wall.

PLAINS HERD – plains herders are from the flat land or plains, in the east of Tornbaer the area is usually called Plains Herd.

DULCEA – A Duchy in Tornbaer usually referred to as the Northern Kingdom it is located on the north of Tornbaer, ruled by Kritchner Debou Bonnard, an area high in riches primarily due to its fertile farmland.

HAUTBAS - area in the duchy of Dulcea, ruled by the Reginald James Cuisinier the second Lord of Hautbas famous for its Coffee Beans.

ROLLSTON - A Duchy to the south of Tornbaer ruled by Duke Hector James Dallinger.

JORN - a small Barony characterised by quiet coastal villages

and little else, it lies in a remote area to the South of
Tornbaer.

SIRILLIA – A large Continent sometimes referred to as the
Western Continent by Kingdom folks as its main port lies to
the West of Bastien, most commonly famous for its alchemy
it is however rich in minerals and metals.

ASTROM - A city on coast of Sirillia, the main seaport, set
out in terraces overlooking the sea, located on the edge of
the Dantallo Desert.

FARTHING CLIFFS – Expansive cliffs east of Astrom, very
dangerous for ships in a storm.

DANTALLO DESERT – One of the many deserts in central
Sirillia

DANTALLO DESERT OASIS – located in the North West of
the Dantallo Desert, home of the Reshda Desert tribe

LEVIRAAN DESERT – Main desert to the North East of
Sirillia

JERONE – town on the edge of the Leviraan Desert

HERO'S END – A tower in the middle of the Leviraan desert
aptly named because none ever return, or if they do never
how they left.

DANAEYE MOUNTAINS – Mountains to the west of
Astrom

ROSE & TICKLE – Rena's Tavern in Crewtown

THE HORNEY SAILOR – Denza's Tavern in Bastien

JUDIAN DESERT – an area of desert to the North West of
Sirilla.

AANLYIS – Home to the Vanglassen, household a small
Barony to the south. Where Bella hails from and learnt
the bow.

TANYE – Port to the North East of Sirillia.

THE CRAGGY ISLES – A large group of islands to the
North of Tornbaer, mostly knowing for high and rocky

country where the residents tend to their Sheep. Said to be the most boring destination in all Mierma.

THINGS

SWINGING SAILOR'S OR FLIGHTIES - Sailors that have been trained at Crewtown, though training includes healing, sail training, flight weaponry and warfare.
THE HOUR OF BLOOD - The hour in which a treasonous act was triggered by Fife Dallinger, during which the previous monarch was killed along with various Kings Guard and Solders of the Kingdom.
DRAGON'S FIRE - An oily substance that is extremely dangerous, could burn nonstop for months, the art of its making has long been forgotten.
LIUYEDAO - Meena's swords, she has two of these she came with them none knows where they come from hers have ribbons on them.
EARLY AGES – A time long ago which little is known about, relics from this age are littered around Mierma such as the North and South Bridges in Bastien and parts of the Citadel, this was a time of great speculation, gear war of magic and might were fought, it was said gods roamed the earth freely and large creatures roamed the realm such as the great lizards. most have forgotten there were ever great mages could build cities and destroy them as well.
YUIANI – An ancient sword technique using katanas and ribbons to kill looks distinctly like dancing.
CROWN - Currency of Tornbaer
SENTINEL CLASS SHIP - A Large Ship mainly used for troop movement relatively slow.
ASCENDER CLASS SHIP – The new generation of Flying Ship courtesy of Marlo's Combustion Chamber invention.
ARA – located at Crewtown, a type of lift that uses a

combustion chamber to raise and lower occupants up and down levels. Goes from the ship platform and the seat of the Barony of Crewtown down to Marlo's workshop and build room, further down is the academy which is sea level.

THE DRAGONS TOOTH – Rorg's ship

THE SERPENT – Castain's Ship

BROTHEL BEAUTY – Bloody Mary's Ship

THE TEMPEST – Morgan Jones ship

CAPTAIN'S BASTARD - Card Game that Pirates like to play, loosely translates on a normal deck, Fool: Joker can't be played last, Captain: 2 Can be any card, Second: Ace, King: King, Queen: Queen, Prince: Jack, 7: 7 but is used to reverse direction, 10-3 normal.

ANEITSU – one of the fighting styles which Morgan has been trained in, it uses an opponent's momentum against them, she was trained by a monk who travelled aboard the Tempest from Sirillia. The Monk was from a temple to the Far north east in a small port called Tanye.

KINGS GUARD – trained in a shield and double-edged longsword style as well as Heavy armour training.

SHORESKIP – Marlo's latest invention.

Mountain Tribespeople – A common term for groups of people who live in roving tribes through the mountains of Tornbaer the largest concentration of which is on the Hanan Mountains. The Dallinger's are their current sovereign, they are never seen at court nonetheless and tend to keep to themselves, skilled at stone cutting, used to build large parts of Huenholme and Crewtown.

ACKNOWLEDGMENTS

Like all the orphans in this book, I was adrift, cast away, left to ponder, that is the state I found myself in in when I wrote this book. Sounds scary but it really was quite the opposite, that is why I would like to acknowledge all those who helped me stay afloat when you could have simply gone about your busy lives, you helped me find a home and a purpose. Thank you especially to Ma and Pa and my Church family who always had my back.

Hey Noel, I really should have ripped the plaster off, but instead you were reminded daily that this book was Marlo's end. Thank you for putting up with my writing exploits and the constant reminders. I promise this is not the end of our animated conversations.